SECRET IDENTITY

Eric pulled Jena toward him. "Oh, Goldilocks, if you knew what kind of a scare you gave me down there. When I looked back and saw you lying in a heap on the rocks. . . ." He shook his head. Suddenly his fingers were entwined in her long, streaming hair, and his lips formed a bond with hers that spoke of his fear . . . and his relief.

All Jena could think as Eric held her tightly was that she'd never been kissed like this before—a real kiss, taking her by surprise, sending her senses spinning, whirling.

But then Eric drew away, his expression uncomfortable, his mouth grim. "I shouldn't have done that."

"Why? I didn't mind."

"Jena, you don't know the half of it. You don't understand."

No, thought Jena sadly. *I really don't understand. I only wish I knew why he's holding back.*

Bantam Sweet Dreams Romances
Ask your bookseller for the books you have missed

Secret Identity

Joanna Campbell

BANTAM BOOKS
TORONTO · NEW YORK · LONDON · SYDNEY

SECRET IDENTITY

A Bantam Book / September 1982

Sweet Dreams is a Trademark of Bantam Books, Inc.

Cover photo by Pat Hill

ISBN 0-553-22683-5

Published simultaneously in the United States and Canada

Bantam Books are published by Bantam Books, Inc. Its trademark,
consisting of the words ''Bantam Books'' and the portrayal of a rooster,
is Registered in U.S. Patent and Trademark Office and in other countries.
Marca Registrada. Bantam Books, Inc., 666 Fifth Avenue, New York,
New York 10103.

PRINTED IN THE UNITED STATES OF AMERICA

O   0 9 8 7 6 5 4 3 2

Secret Identity

Chapter One

The breeze whipped at Jena Maxwell's long, golden hair as she stepped into the glaring afternoon sunlight from the terminal at San Diego Airport. She had made the trip from New York many times before, but with her parents off in Europe, this was the first time she would be spending the summer at the family's cattle ranch, La Paloma, alone. Of course the ranch employees would be there to keep her company—Max Whitney, the ranch manager, Maria and Pepe Juarez, housekeeper and gardener, all of whom had known and loved Jena since she was a toddler. Usually Jena couldn't wait to get to San Diego. She had loved her summers at the ranch and usually looked forward to them eagerly. But this year she felt differently, though she wasn't quite sure why. She would miss her friends back at school, for there were no kids her age within miles of the ranch. Last year when she was fifteen that fact really hadn't bothered her. She had been happy enough to saddle Diablo, the stallion she had raised from a colt, and ride out all day, every day, across the ranch lands. It had always satisfied her, but this summer she knew it wouldn't be enough.

She felt tired and irritable as she squinted into the brightness and scanned the line of cars parked at the curb. She heard a horn to her right and looked over as a green station wagon pulled into a spot. A moment later a tall, wiry man jumped out. He was dressed in jeans and a faded shirt, his worn Stetson pushed back on his head. As he stepped around the car, his weathered face broke into a wide grin.

"Jena! It's good to see you again."

"Max! I was beginning to think you'd forgotten me!"

As Jena hurried forward, she was caught up in a fatherly bear hug. "How are you, Max?"

"Fine, fine."

"And Maria and Pepe?"

"Both great. Looking forward to seeing you."

Max held her for a moment at arm's length. "You're growing up, sweetheart—I don't hardly believe how much! But where's your luggage? Can't believe a young lady your age has come empty-handed. Must have been a few years ago

2

when you didn't care two tinkers what was on your back as long as you were on the back of a horse."

Jena giggled. Max who'd known Jena all her life and had given her her first riding lesson when she was three years old, could tease her all he liked. Fortyish and a confirmed bachelor, he treated Jena like the daughter he'd never had.

"My bags are over there," Jena said, waving toward a pile of luggage. "I had the porter bring them out, and as you can see, I didn't come empty-handed."

Max chuckled as he viewed the luggage. "Yeah, that ought to keep you in jeans the next few months."

"Oh, it's not all clothes. I picked up a few things for you and Maria and Pepe in New York. And then there are my record albums and books and—"

"I get the message. Well, let's get them loaded and head out of here before the traffic starts."

Max loaded the car, then he and Jena climbed in. As Max began maneuvering the wagon out of the airport parking lot, Jena leaned her head back on the seat, sighed, and began to relax. It had been a busy day, and a hectic week leading up to it. First there had been her departure from Chase Girls' School: packing her belongings and cleaning out her room. Her parents had come up to Westchester to help her cart her stuff back to their New York apartment. Then there had been the shopping trips with her mother for a summer wardrobe. Jena had grown over the past year, and very few of her clothes still fit. The shopping had been fun, but it had been exhausting, too. They had no sooner clipped the tags off their purchases when Jena was packing again for her trip to La Paloma and her parents were packing, too, for their departure for Europe.

Jena was disappointed that she wouldn't be going with her parents. True, it was business that called her father to the mountain village in the Swiss Alps. But the conference was for two weeks only, and from there her parents had decided to travel on to France and Italy, visiting old friends for the rest of the summer. As much as Jena had pleaded, they had remained firm. It wasn't a question of their not wanting to spend the summer with their daughter, but they reasoned that, at sixteen, she would be much happier at La Paloma, riding, jumping waves in the nearby ocean, and playing tennis at the local club.

Nothing Jena said could change their decision. She felt frustrated. Yes, she loved La Paloma, but couldn't they realize that she was growing up, that she wasn't their little girl anymore, that she needed excitement, too? After the long year at school, Jena wanted a taste of

4

the outside world, where there would be new faces, parties, concerts, sightseeing.

At sixteen Jena had the deep blue eyes and shining blond hair of her father's family and the high cheekbones and full mouth of her mother. Five-foot-six, she was gracefully built, her body beginning to fill out. What her parents didn't realize was that it wasn't just her body that was changing. Dreams of horses and sand-castles were giving way to thoughts of boys, college, and future plans.

Max's warm, gravelly voice broke into her contemplations. "Added another forty head to the herd this spring. New mare and stallion, too. The mare'll make a good mount for you—a bit wild, but you can handle her."

"How's Diablo?"

"I was wonderin' when you'd ask. He's fit as a fiddle. Be glad to see your face."

Max pulled onto the freeway and headed north. Jena gazed out the window at the exquisite scenery of scrub-covered mountains towering above golden valleys. She caught an occasional glimpse of the blue Pacific in the distance to the left. Here and there a cluster of Spanish, white stucco, red-tile-roofed homes clung to the hill-sides.

Max swung off Route 5, and the station wagon bumped along the roadway for a while, stirring up a cloud of dust. Then up ahead Jena saw the tall stucco entrance posts of La Paloma, with their wrought-iron gates, the tall eucalyptus bordering the drive beyond. The gates were open in expectation of Max and Jena's arrival, and Max drove through.

"How's she look?" He grinned to Jena.

"Wow. I always forget how beautiful it is when I'm away." Yes, it *was* good to be back, despite her worries about spending a lonely summer.

Jena sighed as Max pulled to a halt before the front doors. It was a spectacular sight, a combination of untouched nature and civilization: hints of the past in the stucco ranch house that had seen over two hundred years of history pass through its portals; and signs of the present in the modern equipment used on the farm and in the cattle breeding.

As Jena climbed from the car, the wide front doors of the house swung open, and Maria Juarez burst out, her deep brown eyes snapping with happiness, a wide smile on her face.

"Ah, Jena, it is good to have you back! Come, let me see you. How you have grown!"

Jena hurried up the steps to be enclosed in Maria's warm embrace. Maria was the one who'd always been there when Jena needed her: to bandage a scraped knee, to comfort her when her old pony had broken a leg and had to be put out of his misery, to sneak a treat to Jena's room when she was being punished at age ten for riding off on her pony without permission.

"But why are we standing here on the steps?"

Maria was saying. "Come inside. I have some cool drinks and cake ready." She took one long look at Jena. "What a lovely lady you have become. Such a difference a year makes."

As Max followed with the luggage, Jena and Maria entered the cool, tile-floored entrance hall with its arched doorways and dark-beamed ceiling.

"Come to the kitchen, Max, when you are finished," Maria called. "Pepe is in his garden but will be in later."

She turned to Jena. "I did not ask before, but your mama and papa, they are well?"

"Fine. They're leaving today for Switzerland. They said to say hello to everyone."

"And school? It was good?"

"I can't complain, though I'm glad to be out for the summer."

Jena and Maria walked past the elegantly furnished, spacious living room and the long, formal dining room.

The scent of fresh-baked bread filled Jena's nostrils as she entered the huge, immaculate kitchen. The round wooden table to the side of the room had been set with a checkered cloth, a pitcher of cool fruit punch, and a still warm nut cake that was Maria's specialty. As Maria went to the cabinet for plates and forks, Jena poured herself a tall glass of punch. After the dusty ride in, her throat felt parched.

In a moment Max sauntered into the room,

pulled off his hat, and hung it on one of the wooden pegs beside the door.

"Have a feeling it's going to take you a while unpacking," he said, grinning. "One of them bags must weigh fifty pounds."

"Not that much, Max." Jena laughed. "That bag just has my boots and my record albums in it."

"Some of that jangling rock stuff, no doubt." He shuddered. "Now back in my day, we knew what good music was—a little Tex Ritter. Even that John Denver fella ain't too bad."

"I don't like country and western."

"Just goes to show kids nowadays don't appreciate the finer things in life. And here I was all set to invite you over to the square dance at Rancho Pino. Only have a couple of dances a year, and there'll be some young folks you might like meeting."

Jena perked up. "Now I don't dislike C and W *that* much, and I haven't been to a square dance in at least two years! Of course, the last time no one asked me to dance because I was too young."

"Seems to me I remember Mrs. Jenkins's grandson." Max fingered his chin.

"Oh, him," Jena remarked disgustedly.

"Interested in trying your luck again? Should be better odds. Dance is in a few weeks."

"Sounds good," Jena said as she slid a large piece of cake onto her plate. She was hungrier

8

than she had realized, and after school food, the taste of home cooking was heaven.

They chatted for a while, then Max pushed back his chair. "Well, I thank you for the refreshments, Maria, but I'd best get that wagon put away. Jena, why don't you go down to the stables and check out the horses?"

"I'm not exactly dressed for the stables." She flicked her hand indicating her dress and high heels.

"Horses won't mind, and you'll be in jeans and boots soon enough. I'll meet you down there after I've put away the car. Thanks again for the snack, Maria."

As Max headed around to the front of the house to collect the station wagon, Jena followed the lawns back toward the long, low stable building, then stepped through a gate in the wall surrounding the lawns into the dusty stable yard itself. She paused for a moment at the entrance to adjust her eyes to the darker interior and to take a deep breath of the cool, musky-smelling air. Diablo's stall was the fourth from the end on the left. She saw the stallion's nose pop out over the stall door in curiosity as she approached. His nostrils flared, then he nickered.

"So you haven't forgotten me, fella. You'd better not after all the time we've spent together." She reached out a hand to his neck, then rubbed his soft nose. "Yes, hi, there. Still the same old softie. Sorry, I didn't bring you any treats—just came to say hello." As the stallion nudged Jena's shoulder, Max swung open the wooden stall door.

"Hey there, Jena, come on and take a look at the newest member of Diablo's family."

Diablo arched his neck around as Jena knelt down beside the next stall and gently reached out a hand to a young filly. The filly's fuzzy coat was coal black like Diablo's, and already her spindly frame showed a hint of the fine thoroughbred lines that were her background.

"How old is she?"

"Near to three months. She was a bit undersized when she was foaled, so I thought I'd keep her in the stable here for a while to watch her. Strong enough now, though, and more than caught up to the other foals her age. I'll put her and the mare out in the pasture tomorrow and let them stretch their legs a little."

"I can't believe Diablo's a father. What have you named her?"

"Well, we kinda thought we'd leave that up to you."

"Devil's Daughter," Jena said immediately.

"A mite sinister for such an innocent little thing," Max said doubtfully.

"I named Diablo when he wasn't any bigger."

"And it fits him. OK, Devil's Daughter it will be."

"She'll grow into it, just like he did, and what

else could Diablo's foal be called?" Jena rose and stretched her tired muscles. "Boy, I'm beat. Think I'll go in and relax before dinner. See you later, Max."

"You bet. And, Jena—it's nice to have you back."

"Thanks. It's good to be here." With a wave of her hand and a cheerful, though tired, smile, Jena left for the house. The sun was sinking as she crossed the lawn. Just enough time for a bath and a short rest before dinner.

Chapter Two

After her bath, Jena did lie down, though she didn't sleep. She couldn't seem to stop the thoughts from racing around in her head. She felt funny inside. She kept expecting something to happen . . . something exciting and different. But it was the same as always. Another summer at the ranch. Why didn't she feel happy? Why this restlessness as she looked around her familiar bedroom? Only a year before she could have spent hours hanging around the stables, walking or riding across the pastures, daydreaming, or looking forward to the evening meal, an ice cream sundae, a trip with Max to the nearest town for supplies. Now she felt as though something were missing. Just that afternoon, seeing Diablo and the new filly, she hadn't felt the same excitement as she would have at one time.

She wished there were people her own age to hang out with here, and boys to meet—one boy in particular, although she couldn't picture his face or his coloring. She only knew that the idea of meeting a special boy made her heart start racing. She didn't know too many boys her own age, since she was stuck away in a girls' boarding school during the year and spent holidays and summers at La Paloma, where the only male close to her age was Willie Jenkins, a loudmouthed, bossy kid.

With her close friends from school miles away, Jena felt a real wave of loneliness sweep over her. She was glad when it was dinner time so that she could escape from her thoughts for a while.

As Jena entered the dining room, Pepe, who was already at the table, quickly got up and, beaming, came around the table toward her. For all his husky, broad-shouldered frame, he was still light on his feet.

"Ah, señorita, *cómo está?*" He squeezed her hands as Jena dropped a kiss on his cheek.

Jena laughed. "*Muy bien*, Pepe. It's so good to see you again. I hear your gardens are the pride of La Paloma."

"*Gracias, gracias*, señorita. I try, and the weather has been good—plenty of rain last winter."

"Come, sit." Maria came toward the table with two brimming platters of enchiladas. "Enough time for talk later. Eat while it is hot."

Jena took a deep, appreciative whiff. "Smells fantastic. Do you know that sometimes I sit in the dining room at school and crave just one bite of your cooking?"

Conversation dwindled as the three concentrated on their meal, Pepe digging in after his hard day's labor, Maria concerned whether everything was all right—did Jena want more salad, more sauce?

Finally, her plate clean, Jena leaned back in her chair, feeling contented and lazy. Pepe, too, finished his meal, and Maria began clearing away the dishes, the clatter awakening Jena from her lethargy. "Here, let me help you with those, Maria. Then I have a surprise."

In two trips the table was clear, then Jena motioned Maria into her seat and went to collect her packages.

"What is this?" Maria asked as Jena placed a large, rectangular box in front of her and a smaller one in front of Pepe.

"A little something from New York."

"Oh, Jena, why did you do such a thing?"

"Because I wanted to. Now open them—you first, Pepe."

The man grinned as he untied the ribbon around the package. He tore away the paper and withdrew two books.

"*Qué bien!*" he cried, then read, "*Farmer's Guide to Latest Agricultural Methods* and *Flowers of California. Muchas gracias*, Jena! It is too much."

"Enjoy. I don't know if there's anything in the books that you don't already know, but I thought you'd like them. Now you, Maria."

"Jena, what have you done?" Maria exclaimed as she pulled at the ribbons.

"Nothing you won't love. Look inside."

As Maria opened the box and moved aside the tissue packing, she gave a low sigh of pleasure. She withdrew a delicately patterned, rose silk blouse. "It is lovely . . . lovely."

"Now, if neither of you mind," Jena said, rising, "I'm going to pass on dessert tonight, take a walk around the lawns, and go to sleep. I'm really beat."

Maria and Pepe rose with her, each coming over to give her a hug. "Thank you again."

"You're both welcome. *Buenas noches.* I'll see you in the morning."

"*Buenas noches.* Sleep well."

Jena was sure she would, from pure exhaustion. She had a warm feeling inside, a result of the Juarezes' genuine love, as she stepped out into the early twilight. The air was already cooling now that the sun had set—one of the characteristics of California nights that Jena loved.

She walked across to the Spanish fountain,

sat on its tiled rim for a while, and watched the rippling water. The misty light and sweet evening air made Jena's head swim, and she wondered if maybe, just maybe, something exciting might be around the corner.

Chapter Three

The next morning, the sun brightly slanting through her bedroom shutters woke Jena. She felt refreshed, full of energy as she slid from under the bedcovers and went to the bathroom for a quick shower. Pulling on an old pair of jeans, a light shirt and riding boots, she skipped downstairs for a quick breakfast, then went out to the stables. Max was already in his office when she arrived. Since he normally started his mornings at five, that wasn't surprising. He glanced up from the ledger in front of him as she knocked on the open door.

"Well, good morning there, Jena. You're a might more frisky looking this morning."

"I'm feeling a lot better. I had a good sleep."

"I suppose you'll be wanting Diablo saddled.

Or would you rather go and take a look at the filly first? I put them out in the pasture early this morning. The filly was a little shy at first, but she and her mama are certainly enjoyin' themselves now."

"I thought I'd get Diablo first, then stop by the pasture on my way out."

"Where're you headin'—just in case I have to send a search party out?"

"You don't think I know my way around the place yet?" Jena teased.

"Accidents will happen."

"I'll be riding out toward the coast—maybe to the beach. Should be back by noon."

"OK." Max pushed back his chair. "I'll saddle up Diablo."

"That's all right. I can tack him up myself. And by the way," Jena said, as she brought out a package from behind her back, "this is for you, Max."

Max frowned but accepted the package. "What you got here?"

"Just a little surprise. Gave Maria and Pepe theirs last night and didn't want you to feel left out."

"You shouldn't have." But as the wrappings gave way and Max saw a pipe and his favorite brand of tobacco, he grinned. "You're a real sweetheart, missy. I appreciate it."

"Anytime, Max."

He patted her shoulder awkwardly. "Well, you have a good ride."

"I will. See you later." Tipping the straw, cowboy-style hat she wore to protect her eyes from the sun, Jena strode off to collect Diablo from the stable.

He whinnied when he spotted her, probably anticipating that she had come to take him out for a run. As she led him out of the box stall, she said, "Yes, you're getting your wish, boy. Been awhile since we've been out together."

She had no trouble saddling and bridling him, and in a few minutes they were out of the stable. Mounting, Jena started Diablo in the direction of the small pasture containing the mare and filly. As Jena paused by the fence, she saw the mare in the distance, her head to the ground grazing while the filly frolicked merrily in a circle around her. Diablo lifted his head and gave a loud whinny. The mare looked up, started to come toward them, then changed her mind and resumed grazing.

"Don't worry, old boy." Jena patted Diablo's neck. "We'll stop on the way back, and maybe they'll be more friendly." She nudged the stallion into a trot and moved him out over the open country.

Jena heeled Diablo into a canter, and the animal sprang forward as exhilarated as his rider and as eager to feel the wind rushing against them. Over the rough grass they flew,

19

up the hillside, onto a narrow, dusty cattle trail that would lead them toward the sea.

Diablo was tireless, not once breaking his stride, stretching his long legs at the feel of freedom, his gait eating up the miles. All too soon it seemed to Jena, they reached a crest and could go no farther, for beyond them spread the blue panorama of the Pacific Ocean, gleaming in the sunlight, its frothy white-tipped waves beating against the sandy beach below. The beautiful but isolated stretch of coast a quarter of a mile in each direction was part of the La Paloma Ranch, and Jena loved it. Often in the summer she rode Diablo down here, trotting him along the hard-packed sand at the water's edge as the waves swirled about his hooves.

There were rarely any trespassers on the beach. Max had told her once of the surfing bums he had caught camping on the sand and sent packing, but Jena had never seen anyone.

When she noticed a bit farther down the beach what looked like a figure sprawled on a beach-towel, she was sure she was mistaken. It probably was no more than a piece of driftwood, something washed up by the high tide, but she was curious. She nudged Diablo forward, over the crest and down the sandy, gravelly trail to the beach.

As she drew closer, the figure was unmistakable—a young man, stretched face down on a towel. But what was he doing here?

The deep sand muffled Diablo's hoofbeats and the sound of their approach. They were only a few yards away. Jena saw now that the stranger's broad-shouldered back and long legs were deeply tanned, his body trim and athletic. His face was turned away, but his slightly waving, collar-length, dark hair glistened cleanly in the strong sunlight.

Jena felt a strange excitement at the unexpected turn of events—a nervousness, too, as she wondered if it would be a good idea to make her presence known or turn and ride off, as she was sure Max would have advised her to do. He had always cautioned her about strangers. But she was on horseback—she should be safe enough.

In any case, Diablo took the decision out of Jena's hands by suddenly snorting loudly. The noise was more than enough to startle the figure. He lifted his head and swung around quickly. His eyes widened in disbelief as he saw the legs of a huge black stallion only a few yards away, and on his back a slender girl with long, golden hair.

In one vigorous movement the young man was up and on his feet, standing with his long legs braced, his muscles taut. His expression was that of someone who had been awakened abruptly from a dream and wasn't quite certain of his surroundings.

Jena studied his face—his brown eyes narrowed in a squint, his clean-cut features, his cleft chin, and the firm mouth that at the moment was tightly drawn.

Her heart was beating rapidly; moisture was forming on the palms of her hands where she held the reins. She judged him to be about two or three years older than she was. He was so handsome, she thought. She had never expected the figure on the beach to look anything like this. Although she knew she should say something, she was unable to. All she could do was stare.

Diablo was prancing beneath her, distrustful. Unconsciously, Jena tried to calm him by dropping a soothing hand on his neck. Still the horse pranced, and Jena sat speechless.

"He all right?" The stranger's voice seemed to reverberate in the air. Though his tone had a deep, pleasant ring to it, he seemed shaken, too.

Jena gazed down at the penetrating brown eyes that were staring at her, then looked away nervously, concentrating on Diablo. "He's just high-strung. You startled him when you jumped up."

"I startled *him*?" The stranger's eyes widened in amazement. "What about *me*? Do you usually ride up on your black charger and scare people to death?" The brilliant, white-toothed smile he flashed took some of the edge off his words.

"There's usually no one to scare. This is a private beach."

"Is it? I didn't see any signs. . . ." He raised his hand to shield his eyes.

"People around here know."

"I'm not from the area. Seemed like such a peaceful place, and I like to be alone. Is that why you come here?"

"This beach is part of our ranch, La Paloma."

"I see. Then I guess I'm trespassing. You want me to leave?"

Although it had been Jena's intention all along to tell him to go, suddenly the words didn't come out that way. "How did you find the beach?"

"Easy." He grinned. "I walked out my back door. I'm staying at my friends' place up the coast, Del Costa." He motioned to the right with his arm.

"The Wilder place?" Diablo had quieted, but Jena kept a firm hand on the reins.

"Yeah. Really nice, but it sits on a rock ledge, and this beach looked a lot more inviting."

"Didn't they tell you it was private?"

"They're away. I'm spending a few weeks in the house, keeping an eye on it." The way he stared at her, Jena found it impossible to relax. His eyes held a glint of amusement and admiration, which totally unnerved her. "I've been coming over here the last couple of days," he continued quietly. "I'm surprised I haven't run into you—or don't you ride down here often?"

"Often enough, but I just got in from the East Coast yesterday. I go to school in New York, and I'm only here in the summers."

He shifted his long legs, and the smile was bright again on his face, almost teasing. "I don't bite, you know." And at Jena's blank stare, "You have a look on your face as if you think I'm some kind of a dangerous criminal. Can you smile?"

"Of course I can." She did just that, though a bit unwillingly. "I'm Jena Maxwell."

He seemed delighted with the information. "Nice to meet you. Eric Bliss." He extended his hand. "All right to come close to this guy?"

"He's OK now." As Eric stepped forward, Jena reached down to take his hand. His clasp was firm.

"Sorry about trespassing. I don't usually barge in where I'm not wanted."

"It's all right. You didn't know. Anyway, it's the people who sneak down here, misuse the place, and leave their garbage all over that we want to keep out. I don't think you'd do that."

"I can guarantee I won't. I came down here to get *away* from the crazies, get a little peace and quiet. I don't plan on throwing any wild parties."

24

"Where are you from?"

He hesitated a moment, then said smoothly, "I'm going to school at UC at Berkeley. Originally I'm from Wyoming."

Jena nodded, then frowned. His face seemed so familiar, as if she had met him somewhere before, though that didn't seem likely. She had met so few boys, and she would have remembered meeting him. She shrugged.

"Something wrong?"

"No—it's just that I feel like I know you, like I've seen you somewhere." She laughed. "I guess it's my imagination."

Was it also Jena's imagination that his smile suddenly disappeared, to reassert itself after a startled moment?

"Must be someone who looks like me," he said quickly. "I wouldn't have forgotten you."

Jena blushed at the hint in his voice and nervously brushed the windblown hair from her face.

"So what do you do with yourself all summer besides terrorize the countryside on your horse?"

"For excitement, not much unless I go up to L.A. or down to La Jolla or San Diego. No kids around. I do a lot of riding, play tennis, come down here to swim."

"When there aren't any trespassers," he said, "like myself."

"Actually you're the first person I've run into."

"But I shouldn't make a habit of coming over."

His eyes looked into hers questioningly, and Jena made up her mind in that instant that she wasn't going to chase him away, not even if Max had a fit when he learned she had given permission to someone to use their beach. She had never met a boy like him.

"Come—anytime you like." Her voice sounded breathless even to her own ears. "It'll be all right."

"You're sure?"

"Positive."

"Maybe I'll take you up on it."

For a moment they stared at each other silently. Then Diablo began prancing again, breaking the spell. Jena tried to calm him, but Eric motioned to her. "I think your horse wants to be moving on, and I'd better get going, too. My stomach's talking to me—I haven't had any lunch."

"It was nice to meet you." Jena didn't want the conversation to end, yet she didn't have much choice.

"You, too." He gave the stallion's neck a quick pat and stepped back. "Take care of yourself, Goldilocks."

She giggled. "Goldilocks? She didn't ride a horse."

"I know. I was talking about the hair. Any objections?"

"No . . ."

26

He looked serious for a moment, then his broad smile flashed again. "Good. Better get that monster moving before he decides to trample me to death. Catch you later, Goldilocks."

"Bye, Eric." But her words were swept away as Diablo, in his impatience to be off, swung around and with little encouragement from Jena cantered down the beach.

Chapter Four

As the stallion and the girl disappeared across the sand, Eric Bliss stood staring after them. The last thing he had expected when he'd come to the beach that day was to meet a girl—a blond-haired beauty at that, charging up on a black horse, intriguing him with the suddenness of her arrival. He had found himself instantly attracted to her, to her loveliness and the shy warmth of her personality; he felt the urge to see her again and get to know her better.

He shook his head distractedly; a frown appeared on his brow as he reminded himself that he shouldn't let anything happen. This wasn't just a quiet vacation for him. It was a temporary escape from the rock music world—a world in which there was no such thing as a private life; where hungry fans shadowed his every footstep, their enthusiasm at times endangering his personal safety; where to get any peace he had to hide away, stay far from the crowds, adopt an assumed identity.

He wasn't the college student he had led Jena to believe. He wasn't even Eric Bliss. He was Eric Clayton, rock star, lead guitarist of the successful and popular Ravens. Posters of his face were plastered on the bedroom walls of teenage girls all over the country. And his disguise had been necessary.

He had come to the beach house on the isolated bit of coastline for a month or two during a break in the Ravens' concert schedule. He hadn't expected to meet anyone. In fact, he'd gone out of his way to make sure he didn't, hiring a housekeeper, an older woman who had no idea of his real identity, to run errands, cook his meals, answer the telephone. He'd had no plans except to stick close to the beach house, lie in the sun, swim, get his head back on straight, and recoup his energy before heading back to Los Angeles at the end of August to rejoin the Ravens for some recording sessions and another tour. He had been perfectly content by himself for the last few days with no human contact except for his housekeeper. He had missed nothing; in fact, he had relished the peace and quiet.

29

Then she had arrived. Maybe he'd been a fool to leave the Del Costa grounds, but the empty beach had seemed so perfect. He liked her, liked talking to her. He had never known a girl to make such a strong and sudden impression on him, and he enjoyed the fact that she had met him as a regular person, not as a glitter-studded star. It had made him realize how much he missed having a private life. He had hated lying to her, but he'd had no choice. He was amazed she hadn't recognized him. His heart had climbed in his throat when she had said he looked familiar, and he had breathed a very thankful sigh when she had believed his cover story. All he needed was for one innocent remark to reach the wrong set of ears, and his hideaway wouldn't be a hideaway any more.

Jena and her horse were only a speck in the distance as they climbed the hill away from the beach. He thought he saw her looking back over her shoulder, but she was too far away for him to be sure. He wondered if she would come back the next day or the next. Despite her offer, it would be wiser if he didn't come back himself.

As he reached down to grab his towel, he wondered, as he had several times in the past, if the price he had to pay for fame was worth it. He had made it through the worst, he supposed. When he'd first come to Los Angeles at sixteen to begin his college education and gotten hooked up with an amateur rock group at UCLA, he'd been an innocent kid. True, as a talented guitarist, he had played with a couple of groups back home in Wyoming, but that had been small-town stuff. The big-time music scene was a whole different ball game, with all new rules, and he'd really been thrown into it. When a friend had put him on to the audition for the Ravens, he'd gone for the heck of it, expecting nothing. The Ravens were already pretty well known, about to cut their second album, and Eric wasn't sure he had the stuff to make the grade. But he'd had it, and a week later he was rehearsing with them, dropping out of UCLA and getting ready to go on tour.

That was two years ago. Eric had walked around with his head in the clouds for months. The album he had cut with the Ravens hit the top of the charts; the Ravens were in demand for concerts, for appearances. At first the screaming fans, the publicity, the sight of his face staring back at him from magazine articles had been an ego trip. How could anyone get tired of this? he had wondered. Then the harsher reality had begun settling in. First had been the realization that he could no longer jump in his car for a ride along the beach or for a quick hamburger. The Ferrari, the car of his dreams that he'd never imagined he could afford, had sat in a garage. If he took it out, someone would spot him; there would be a mob scene. Yet that had been mild compared to some of the other aspects of the music world: the wild, reckless life-style, the drinking, the drugs. Somehow he'd managed to survive, stay on the outside edges of it all, though the pressure on him had been terrific. None of it was part of the scene Eric had been used to. Sure, there had been drugs in Wyoming, but he had had enough sense to know the dangers and had never wanted or needed to have his head messed up. The other Ravens had finally accepted his opinions, and in the end, he had had a good effect on all of them. Their shows only got better, and even Tod, the drummer, who'd gotten really messed up a couple of times, was straightening out.

The only part of Eric's new life he hadn't been able to get used to was the exhaustion brought on by months on the road, long concerts that could drain every ounce of energy from his body, and the pressure of being on top and staying there, producing, recording, and coming up with new sounds that the fans would love.

Of course, Eric wasn't ready to quit. He loved it—the excitement, the cheering audience, and, above all, the music. Music was in his blood.

Now as he started off down the beach, his footprints leaving a trail in the wet sand, Eric suddenly felt nervous about the way Jena had made his blood race. He couldn't stop thinking about her. But much as it brought a nice feeling, it was no good. There was no place for romance in his secret life. He didn't want to expose himself. Or expose her to the wildness of his world. He was crazy to consider it. He had no choice but to play it cool.

Chapter Five

As Diablo thundered up the slope away from the beach, Jena looked back once, quickly, over her shoulder. He was still there, watching her. Eric Bliss. She couldn't believe that the morning had turned out so fantastically. This was just the sort of thing she had been waiting for, the kind of chance meeting that had filled her dreams but had seemed too farfetched to become reality. Funny, though—a young guy like that taking a vacation all by himself. Jena couldn't figure out why he wasn't living it up someplace, the way she would have liked to do. She sighed out loud. He was so handsome. She loved his cleft chin, the sparkle in his dark eyes when he smiled, his easy way of talking, and his casual self-confidence. If only she could have been as confident of herself. She had been so nervous when they had started talking. Had it shown? She couldn't even remember what she had said, whether she had stumbled over her words; yet all his answers were clearly etched in her mind. And he'd called her Goldilocks. She liked that. It must mean he was interested. Or was it only part of his friendly manner?

She wanted to see him again. He had said he might take her up on her offer to use the beach again, but would he show? Would she ride down tomorrow and the next day and the next, only to find an empty stretch of sand? She didn't want to think of that possibility—not now. She didn't want anything to ruin this feeling of excitement.

The ranch was deserted when Jena got back. She cooled down Diablo and let him into the corral. Max and the hands were out on the range, Pepe in the village. Maria was busy in the kitchen baking and in no mood for a chat. Jena wasn't sure if she wanted to talk to anyone about her morning just yet anyway. She wanted Eric to be hers alone for just a little longer.

Jena grabbed a quick lunch. Then, when Pepe came back, she asked him if he would drive her to the country club so that she could play some tennis. He agreed, and she quickly changed into her tennis clothes. When she went outside, he was already in the car, waiting.

The club was nestled in a valley off the main road a few miles west of the ranch. On the weekends when people traveled out from the cities, it was a busy place, but during the week there were only a few members on the court and in the pool. She hoped she'd be able to find a partner, but if not, at least she could put her name up on the board and maybe have an hour's lesson with the tennis coach.

Pepe dropped her off, and she arranged a time for him to pick her up. Then she walked over toward the courts. She saw the coach leaning against the court fence talking to a girl about her own age. When he saw Jena approaching, he gave her a friendly wave.

"Well, hello there. Good to see you back."

"Hi, Coach Miles. How're things?"

"Great. Out for a little tennis?"

"If I can find a partner."

"Your timing couldn't be more perfect. Jena, I'd like you to meet Susan Strasberg. Her family just moved into the old Peterson place. Susan, this is Jena Maxwell of the La Paloma Ranch. Susan's also looking for a partner. Maybe the two of you could team up."

Susan was a pretty, petite brunette, her long hair drawn back into a ponytail at the back of her neck. She smiled at Jena. "Nice to meet you."

"You, too." Jena smiled back, surprised and

happy to see someone else her own age. "Like to play a couple of sets?"

"Sure. I'm really glad you came along."

"Then I'll leave you two on your own," Coach Miles said, striding off toward the clubhouse as the girls moved toward the court.

Jena began unzipping her racket cover. "Where are you from originally?"

"Los Angeles. Encino, actually. Dad still spends a lot of time up there with his business, but the rest of us will be here year round."

"How do you like it?"

"So far, OK. Of course, I really miss my friends in Los Angeles. I was kind of afraid there wouldn't be any kids my age here, but now I've met you. You live here year round, too?"

"Only summers. We live in New York the rest of the year, and I go to school there."

"That must be fun! You sure don't get bored."

"Well, sometimes. I go to a private school, and they're pretty strict, but you're right about there not being many kids our age around here."

"So what do you do for excitement?" Susan took a ball from the tennis can she was carrying.

"This is it." Jena swept out her arm indicating the courts and pool. "And I do a lot of riding. Do you ride?"

"A little. I'm learning, actually. Dad got a couple of saddle horses."

"We should get together sometime."

"Love to. I'll give you my phone number before we leave."

"Vice versa. You ready?"

The girls had reached opposite sides of the court, and Jena told Susan to serve first.

They turned out to be well matched. The two sets they played were energetic and fast paced. They were both perspiring and flushed from the heat and exercise when they decided to call it quits.

"Thanks—good game," Susan called as they met at the end of the net. "How about a soda?"

"I could use one."

They got a couple of sodas from the machine outside the clubhouse and sat down at one of the umbrella-shaded tables.

"How often do you come over to play?" Jena asked, taking a long drink.

"This is my first time, but I thought I'd play Thursday again and maybe try the pool."

"Want a partner?"

"Love it."

"Great. I'll see you then. Oh, and here's my number." Jena dug into her bag for a piece of paper and pen, scribbled down the number, then handed the paper to Susan, who was doing likewise. After exchanging numbers, Susan rose.

"I'd better be going. Just got my license this year, and they'll probably be worried at home if I'm gone too long."

"Lucky you," Jena said enviously. "In New York State the driving age is seventeen, not sixteen like it is in California. I've still got a few months to go."

"Too bad," Susan said sympathetically. "Can I give you a ride home?"

"Thanks, but I've already arranged for someone to come and get me."

"Well, at least I can pick you up on Thursday," Susan said. "I'll give you a call before then."

"Great."

Susan slung her bag over her shoulder, then grabbed her racket. "I've got to go. If I don't get home, my mom will be having a fit. Every time I leave the house I get a fifteen-minute lecture. Be careful, drive slowly, don't do this, watch out for that, if you get a scratch on the car Daddy will have a fit." She giggled. "Funny thing is, I'm a better driver than my mother. She's awful—she tore the trim off the garage door in Encino three times before Dad finally told her to just leave the car parked in the drive."

"Did she really?" Jena laughed. "I'd be embarrassed to get behind the wheel after that."

"Doesn't faze her. She always blames it on something—my brother's bike was in the way, the sun was in her eyes." Susan shrugged impishly. "See you Thursday."

"Sure will."

As Jena watched Susan walk away, she thought about what a fantastic day it had turned out to be. All these unexpected surprises—meeting both Eric and Susan. The summer suddenly seemed full of promise.

Chapter Six

Jena had Diablo saddled by eleven-thirty the next morning. She was up much earlier but spent time talking to Maria and going out to the pasture to watch the filly and give her bits of apple. She didn't want to seem too eager, riding down to the beach, even if it was the foremost thought on her mind. Would he come? Maybe he'd wait for afternoon. Maybe he wouldn't be as nice as last time. Maybe she was being foolish riding down there at all. But she had to go; she couldn't ignore that scary, wonderful, racing feeling inside her.

If they took their time, she and Diablo wouldn't be at the beach until noon. Jena mounted and headed Diablo out of the stable yard. She kept his pace slow, though the stallion fidgeted, anxious to stretch his long legs. Over the golden hills they trotted, Jena following a longer, winding route. Then they were on the same hilltop, looking down at the Pacific. For a moment Jena was afraid to look. She took a deep breath, then slowly let her gaze slide along the beach.

He was there, lying on the sand, face up this time, though his head was turned away. In the next instant Jena was urging Diablo down the slope, cantering across the beach, then slowing to a trot and skidding to a halt a short distance from Eric.

He rolled to his side, looked up with twinkling eyes, and smiled. "I heard you this time, Goldilocks. No more surprises. Didn't think you were coming today."

"I had some things to do." It was only a partial lie, and she didn't feel guilty.

"Why don't you come down off your charger and talk to me for a while? You've got an unfair advantage up there on his back."

Gracefully dismounting, Jena stood by Diablo's head, holding the reins. She felt uncomfortable again with Eric gazing up at her in his self-assured way, a crooked grin on his lips.

He sat up leisurely and brushed a few stray bits of sand from his shoulders. "So what were you doing that kept you so busy this morning? You help out at the ranch?"

"If I feel like it, but there are plenty of hands. Max keeps everything running smoothly. Actually I was looking after the new filly. Diablo became a father this spring."

"Did he? Must be a good-looking filly."

"She's cute, but since I've named her Devil's Daughter, she's going to have to live up to it."

"Like father, like daughter." Eric got to his feet and eyed Diablo. "Want to walk for a while so he doesn't get restless?"

"Sure, if you'd like."

"Down there by the water," he said. "It's easier going and better than this hot sand on my feet."

He came to walk beside her as she led Diablo along. Until Eric had stood, she hadn't realized just how tall he was, but the top of her head reached only slightly above his shoulder. Since Jena was fairly tall herself, she knew that Eric had to be over six feet.

"I like your hat." He reached out and touched a finger to the brim of her straw, cowboy-style hat.

"Oh, thanks. Helps to keep the sun out of my eyes." Jena didn't know how she managed to answer so casually; her heart was beating like crazy.

"Used to have one something like it in Wyoming when I helped my Dad with the cattle. The other guys used to rib me to death and wanted to know if I was trying out for the local fashion show, but the straw's a lot cooler than felt."

"You know ranching? You ride?" Jena was amazed.

"Sure do. Since I was old enough to walk. My parents have a big spread outside Laramie."

"You're kidding! I never would have guessed."

"I don't look the cowboy type, huh?" He laughed.

"Well, I didn't mean that as an insult—it's just that you seem so sophisticated. Not like the hands at the ranch, who turn red if I so much as say good morning to them."

"Can you blame them?"

It was Jena's turn to blush.

"We did have schools in Wyoming, you know. Besides, I wasn't a hand. My parents owned the place. It's a little different—just like it is for you."

"You said you're going to Berkeley?"

"Mmmm." They had reached the water's edge now and the cool, moist sand.

"What are you majoring in?"

"Engineering." That wasn't really a lie, Eric decided, since engineering had been his goal at UCLA before he had gotten hooked up with the Ravens and decided to make music his career.

"Not much use for engineering on a ranch, is there?" Jena asked.

"Well, I wasn't planning on going back to the ranch for good. I have an older brother who'll probably take over when Dad retires."

"Oh."

44

"What do you want to do with your life?"

Jena was silent for a moment. "I really don't know. I like art, and I'm pretty good at it, but I'm not sure I have the patience to be a success at it. Mom and Dad say I have enough time to decide when I get into college."

"How old are you?"

Jena was almost startled by his question and hated to tell, since he was obviously older. "Sixteen."

"Still in high school? A junior?"

"Senior in the fall. I go to a private school and have enough credits to get out a year early."

She was puzzled by his suddenly serious expression. Was it her age that bothered him?

But then he smiled. "Funny, it seems like such a long time ago now that I got on that plane for California . . . my mother standing there with tears in her eyes like she'd never see me again."

"You weren't away from home much as a kid?"

"We used to travel together, but Dad couldn't stay away from the ranch for long."

Jena wondered why Eric wasn't spending his vacation with his family, but she felt she might be prying if she asked, so she said nothing.

"Your parents come out here with you every summer?" Eric's voice broke into her thoughts.

"This summer they're in Europe. They sent me out here because they thought I'd have been bored with them."

45

"Would you?"

"Are you kidding? I would have loved to have gone! I begged them to take me. I was there before when I was younger, but it would have been different now."

"How different?"

"Well, I'm older. I thought maybe I could go to some of the parties. . . ." She lowered her eyes. "You know."

"Yeah, I know." His voice sounded almost scornful. "But being here is a heck of a lot healthier, believe me."

What a strange thing for him to say, Jena thought. Did he have something against having fun? What was Eric's story?

They had walked almost to the end of the beach to the cliffs that formed a barrier between La Paloma and the next property down the coast.

"You have to get home for lunch?" Eric asked.

"Guess so."

"We'd better head back."

"Why don't you come with me?" The words were out of her mouth before Jena even knew it.

"Come with you?" He looked at her.

"Back to the ranch—for lunch."

He frowned. "I don't know. . . ."

"I guess you have other things to do." Jena tried to keep the disappointment from her voice.

"No . . . I mean—"

46

"We could go riding after. You still like to ride?"

"Sure—but listen. How are the people at your place going to like you coming in with a stranger?"

"Oh, they won't mind, and you'll be Max's friend for life if you know something about ranching."

Eric looked down and made circles in the sand with his toe as he stalled for time. He wanted to go, but he knew he shouldn't. Finally, he gave a grin. "Well, if you think it's all right. . . ."

As he walked down the beach with her to collect his towel, jeans, and shirt, he wondered if he was nuts. What was wrong with him? Here he'd set out to keep things cool, and what was he doing but riding home for lunch with her. Somehow he couldn't get his common sense to work. He quickly rationalized: it was only for lunch and a ride. Nothing would come of it.

As they reached his towel and Eric climbed into his jeans, he hesitated and looked over at her. "Wait a minute. How far of a walk is it to your ranch? I didn't bring any shoes."

Jena threw back her head in laughter. "You weren't planning on walking, were you? You'll ride up behind me."

"On him?" Eric's eyes widened. "Listen, I know horses, and I know he's not the kind to take to everyone."

"He'll be fine. I promise. And one of the guys

at the ranch should be able to lend you a pair of boots when we go riding later."

"You've got all the answers, don't you, Goldilocks?" He grinned as he buttoned his shirt. Then, grabbing his towel, he said, "I just hope I don't end up with a broken collarbone. Okay, mount up. I'll swing up behind—and hope luck's with me today."

But Diablo, in fact, stood very patiently as Eric swung himself into the saddle behind Jena.

"See, what did I tell you?" she couldn't help commenting.

"Just keep it slow." His voice came from behind her ear. "This isn't the most comfortable seat."

"You bet."

She felt the hard warmth of his chest, against her back, and it was an overpowering sensation. She took a deep breath, silently ordering her rapidly beating heart to slow down, as Diablo started forward at a walk.

Chapter Seven

Max was in the stable yard when they rode in. Jena had told him about her meeting with Eric and how she had told Eric it was OK to use the beach. Max hadn't been entirely happy; he looked less happy now as he saw Eric on the back of Jena's saddle.

Jena called out quickly. "Max, this is Eric Bliss—the guy I told you about yesterday. We started talking, and I asked him over for lunch."

"That so." Max waited, frowning, until Eric dismounted and stepped forward.

"Eric," Jena continued, "this is Max Whitney, our ranch manager."

Eric took Max's hand. "Glad to meet you. Sorry to barge in like this."

"So you're staying at the Wilder place."

"For a few weeks, keeping an eye on things."

Jena swung off Diablo and walked forward. "Eric's a cattleman, too, Max. He was brought up on a ranch in Wyoming."

"Were you," Max said dryly, not yet sure what to make of Eric. "Big spread?"

"Couple thousand acres."

Max's eyebrows lifted. "How many head you runnin'?"

"Used to run seven or eight hundred and some horses, but I've been away the last two years, and I'm not sure what Dad's doing now."

That's funny, thought Jena. *I wonder why he never goes back to see his parents.*

"Breed Hereford?" Max was asking.

"And Black Angus."

Jena decided it was time to interrupt the cattle talk. "Eric and I were thinking of taking a ride after lunch. One small problem, though. He didn't bring his boots to the beach, so he'll need to borrow a pair."

"Noticed."

"Think one of the hands has an old pair laying around?"

"See what I can do. What size you wear?" Max eyed Eric. "About eleven?"

"On the nose."

"Then I probably got a pair of my own I can lend you."

"I'd appreciate it." Eric smiled.

Max nodded. "You'll be ridin' Diablo again, Jena?" When she said yes, he eyed Eric. "You're a good rider, I take it."

"Haven't been up much in the last two years, but I used to be."

"Don't forget that fast. I'll give you Buckthorn. When you headin' out? And where you goin'?"

"After we eat. I thought I'd take him over the ranch, up to Lost Canyon."

"Well, you know your way around. Just be careful. If you're not back by five, I'll come out looking." He glanced back to Eric. His expression clearly warned Eric to behave himself. Since that was part of Eric's plan, too—to be careful, keep his distance—he was able to look Max straight in the eye.

"I'll make sure we get back early."

Max tipped his ranch hat. "Well, go find Maria and get something to eat. I'll have the horses ready when you come out."

"Thanks, Max." Jena squeezed her old friend's arm, her eyes saying silently, "This guy's all right. You don't have to worry."

The introduction with Maria went much more easily. Maria hadn't forgotten what it was like to be a girl Jena's age. And besides, her woman's intuition told her Eric was a decent guy.

Eric and Jena munched on sandwiches, and each had a piece of Maria's delicious cake. Then they went back out to the stables. Max had the two horses saddled and tied to the corral rail in the shade of a cottonwood.

He emerged from his office with boots and a pair of socks. "See how they fit." He handed them to Eric, who sat down on the ground and pulled on the socks, then the boots. He stood up, wiggled his toes, and took a few steps. "Okay. Broken in, too. Thanks a lot."

"No problem. You two be careful out there." Again the warning to Eric was in his eye. The young man understood.

Eric felt good as he sank into the saddle. It had been a long time, but his roots were here. Although he would never give up his musical life, he missed riding out across the open countryside, the sun on his back.

As they rode, Eric glanced at Jena, perfectly comfortable on Diablo. She had to be a good rider to handle a horse like that. She smiled at him.

He grinned back. "I didn't realize you had a place like this."

"What were you expecting? I said it was a cattle ranch."

"I was picturing a place like back home: no fancy finishing touches, just a ranch house, plain and simple, bunkhouses within shouting distance, a little patch of flowers—certainly no housekeeper."

"Maria's the best. She and her husband have been here for years. They're like family."

"So tell me more about yourself. You have any brothers or sisters?"

"No. I've often wished I did. It gets lonely. How about you? You said you have an older brother."

"And sister. She's married to a doctor and lives in Massachusetts. I'm the baby."

"Babies are supposed to be the spoiled ones," Jena said, teasing.

"Not me. My father's favorite expression was, 'Spare the rod and spoil the child.' Not that we ever got hit much—the threat was enough. He had this strap hanging in the kitchen. All he had to do was look at it, and, boy, did we fall in line!" He laughed. "And we all had our share of work to do around the ranch. My parents said that if we wanted something, we had to work for it. I hated it when my buddy's parents bought him a car, and I had to break my butt delivering hay and grain before I could save up enough to buy my own. But I'll tell you one thing. I appreciated that beat-up old heap a lot more than he appreciated his new one. I took better care of mine, too."

"For all he's given me, my father feels the same," Jena said. "He says he had to use his brains to get where he is today—no one handed him anything on a silver platter—and he expects me to do the same."

"Makes sense. Believe me, I've seen how too

much money and getting things too easily can blow people apart." Eric was frowning as though his words brought unpleasant memories. Jena was about to ask him what he meant by that, when Eric suddenly looked over at her. "You're nice—you know that?" he said.

"You're pretty nice yourself." Jena smiled shyly. Her cheeks felt warm.

"Oh, I don't know about that." Eric laughed. "Don't let your first opinions fool you. Come on, I'll race you up that next trail. There should be a beautiful view from the other side."

"There is."

"Let's go."

"Diablo's the better horse," Jena warned.

"That may be, but I know a few tricks."

They galloped up the dusty trail. Eric was a good rider; Jena couldn't believe how good. He had Buckthorn climbing the incline as though he'd ridden the horse for years instead of less than an hour.

Diablo snorted as they surged ahead. He suddenly gained more power; his long legs stretched. But Buckthorn's shorter, more sure-footed gait was better suited to the mountain trail, and Eric knew how to handle him.

As they reached the crest of the trail and the small, brown-grassed meadow, Diablo had pulled up to Buckthorn's neck. Jena knew he would take the other horse in the flat stretch, but Eric was already pulling up, circling around, a wide grin on his face. "Told you I'd give you a run for your money."

"We could have passed you," Jena called breathlessly, "across this stretch."

"Why do you think I stopped?" He laughed. "It's called quitting while you're ahead."

"No fair!"

"The race was to the top of the trail," he reminded her.

"OK, I know when I'm beaten, but next time you won't find it so easy."

"Don't worry, I'll be the loser tomorrow. After not being in the saddle for so long, I'm going to be hurting."

Eric was looking out over the landscape spread below them. "Wow, what a view! This is something. You can even see the ocean from up here."

"It's one of the highest points on the ranch. I love to come up here."

"I sure can see why. I always liked heights myself." He sat for a moment, staring out, then turned. "What's over here?" He started across to the opposite side of the meadow.

"That's where I was going to take you. It leads down into Lost Canyon, but watch out, the trail's real steep and rocky. We can follow it along the bottom of the canyon for about half a mile, then there's another trail that will take us up on the opposite side. About a hundred years ago they say a gang of rustlers hung out in the canyon here, but I don't believe it."

"Why not? Looks like a good hiding spot."

"I've never found any signs of civilization down there, and you'd think they would have left something behind—pans or bottles or tools."

"They might have been washed away or been covered by rubble. Looks like there've been a few landslides."

"A few winters ago, during the heavy rains. Max said some cattle had wandered in here, and they had a heck of a time getting them out."

Eric started down. "Well, watch your step."

"You, too."

The ground was dry and crumbly as they eased the horses slowly down the narrow, winding track. Every so often a stone would be knocked loose by the horses' hooves, and it would go bouncing down to the canyon floor below. Jena wasn't worried. She had been down the trail so many times in the past that she knew it was safe. In a few minutes they had reached the canyon bottom, where the trail looped back on itself to follow a dried-up stream.

"They should have called this echo canyon," Jena said as she eased Diablo up on Buckthorn's flank. "If you call out from this end, your voice will come back at you."

"I don't know how smart that would be—" Eric began.

Jena cut him off. "Listen." She cupped her hands around her mouth, then called out loudly, "Hello, Eric." And sure enough echoing back at them came, "H-e-l-l-o, E-r-i-c."

"Wait, Jena. There's a lot of loose rock and gravel up there, and the vibration of your voice could be all that's needed to set it all rolling."

"No way." Jena laughed. "I've called out echoes hundreds of times, and nothing's happened."

"Let's not test our luck."

"Chicken." She giggled.

Suddenly there was a clattering noise, a distant knocking of rock on rock, increasing in intensity, becoming a rushing noise.

Simultaneously Eric and Jena looked up.

"Geez!" he cried. "Jena, get moving as fast as you can. Hurry up!" With a slap of his hand, Eric had Buckthorn moving at top speed over the rough ground. Jena needed no encouragement to get Diablo to follow. The horses whinnied nervously and fought for their footing on the rocky ground as they bounded ahead.

The mass of sliding stone and gravel was halfway down the canyon wall, making a deafening noise.

"Can we make it, Eric?" Jena's breathless voice reflected her fear.

"I think so. Stay with me!"

Between their horses' panic and their own, everything seemed to move in slow motion. Jena saw the spot ahead where they would be out of the range of the slide, yet in her mind's eye, it seemed they were making no progress. And the rocks were coming closer and closer.

Eric clattered up a slight grade, looking back to see if Jena was with him. Diablo's eyes were rolling wildly, his nostrils were flaring, yet he surged forward, up beside Buckthorn.

Jena heard Eric's escaped breath of relief, but she was afraid to look back over her shoulder. Her heart was pounding like a hammer in her chest.

"The further up the canyon we go, the better." Eric continued to push Buckthorn forward. "This thing could set off a chain reaction."

Jena kept her eyes straight ahead, intent only on staying with Eric. Then suddenly a single rock bounced off the canyon wall directly in front of Diablo. In wild panic, the horse reared and neighed. Jena went flying through the air. The jar as she hit the rock-covered ground seemed to tear her bones apart. The wind was knocked out of her, and she could only lie there on her back, gasping, waiting for the rest of the rocks and gravel she was sure were coming to smother her, bury her alive.

But everything was very still and silent, ominously so. She could hear Eric, his voice ringing in the air. "Jena, oh, no." Then he was kneeling down beside her, lifting her head. "You all right?"

She managed a weak nod. "I think so. . . ."

"You've scraped your face."

She winced as he touched her cheek.

"Sorry." His eyes were anxious with worry. "Do you think you can get up? We've got to get out of here before the whole thing goes. Here, let me help you."

At another time Jena might have melted as his strong arms closed about her and lifted her to her feet. Now she only felt relief at the sound of his heartbeat where her cheek pressed against his chest.

With his arm supporting her, he moved quickly toward Buckthorn, who was standing nervously but steadily a few feet away.

"Thank heavens for a well-trained pony," Eric muttered under his breath as he helped her into the saddle.

"Where's Diablo?"

"Took off with the wind on his heels." Eric swung himself quickly into the saddle behind her as he grabbed the reins. "Let's get out of here!"

"I can't believe Diablo panicked like that," Jena said, her voice trembling.

"That's what comes from too much thorough-bred blood—too high-strung," Eric said tensely. "Not like this baby here. Come on, Buckthorn," he called urgently as he prodded the horse over the rocks and up the trail that would take them out of the canyon. "Show me your stuff."

He didn't ease up on the pace until they reached the crest of the canyon.

A distinct rumbling could be heard behind them. Eric turned Buckthorn, and he and Jena watched in horror as the whole side of the canyon wall seemed to give way, covering the area where they had been moments before.

Jena was shaking. She couldn't stop herself as she realized that if it hadn't been for Eric, she would have been beneath that pile.

Within seconds all was silent again; there was only a brownish cloud of dust rising from Lost Canyon floor as evidence of what had just occurred.

"My God," whispered Jena. "I don't believe . . ."

"You've got to rest awhile." Eric's voice was quiet as he dismounted. "So do I."

He reached up his arms for her and helped her to the ground. Jena's legs nearly buckled. They felt like rubber, unwilling to support her weight. Eric grasped her around the waist.

"You're hurt!"

"No—only thinking if I'd been alone. . . ." Her eyes, still wide from fright, gazed up at Eric.

The firm set of his mouth told her he had been thinking the same thought.

Suddenly his other arm went around her, and he pulled her close. "Oh, Goldilocks, if you knew what kind of a scare you gave me down there. When I looked back and saw you lying in a heap on the rocks. . . ." He shook his head quickly. They clung together for a moment, then Jena lifted her head.

"Eric—thank you."

He was staring at her, his face, his eyes, his lips so close. "That's OK, Goldilocks." His voice was unsteady. "We've got to get you back and doctored up. That scratch on your cheek—"

"It's all right—it doesn't hurt."

"You're probably in shock. Let me look at it." He turned her face gently and examined the cuts. "I don't even have a handkerchief to clean off the blood."

"Am I bleeding?"

"A little." His expression was concerned. He pulled his shirt out of his jeans and using the bottom of it dabbed at her cheek. "It could have been a lot worse."

Jena said nothing, silently thrilled by the gentle touch of his hands.

"There, that's better," he said.

Jena looked up at him, her eyes liquid.

Eric saw the look, was moved by it, and suddenly his fingers were tangling in the long, golden hair streaming down her back. He pulled her close again. His head dropped; his mouth found hers. His lips formed a bond with hers that spoke of his fear . . . his relief.

All Jena could think as she was held tightly in his arms was that she had never been kissed like this before—a real kiss, which took her by surprise, sending her senses spinning, whirling.

But suddenly Eric drew away, his expression uncomfortable, his mouth grim. "I shouldn't have done that."

"Why?"

"I just shouldn't have. It was wrong of me."

"I didn't mind." She smiled. "Really."

"Jena, you don't know the half of it. You don't understand." He shook his head sadly, but there was a warmth in his eyes. "Let's head back. Do you think you can ride?"

"We've got to find Diablo." Jena felt confused; she couldn't sort out what was happening, what had just happened.

Eric motioned with his head over her shoulder. "He's right over there, looking like the guilty coward he is."

Jena turned, and the stallion, standing a few yards away, his head hanging, nickered and began walking forward.

"He's never been a coward."

"He had every reason, I guess," Eric added.

When Diablo was within a few feet, Jena reached out a hand and stroked his nose. The stallion nudged her. "Yes, we all had a scare, fella."

"Don't be so easy on him." Eric put his arm around her. "Do you want to come up with me instead of riding him back?"

"He'll be all right."

"He's not the one I'm worried about. You're still shaking."

She couldn't tell him that it was his arm around her that had her trembling more than the memory of their near disaster. She just looked at him, and he seemed to read the thoughts in her mind.

"Maybe you're right, Goldilocks, and you should try to make it back on your own."

Before she could speak, Eric released his hold on her, leaving only a gentle hand on her arm. "How're your legs? Walk a few steps." He led her in a small circle.

"They seem to work." She smiled unsteadily.

"But they're going to take one look at you at the ranch and go into a panic—scratched, bleeding, covered with dirt, your hair all tangled. And you've lost your hat."

"Oh—I didn't even realize it."

"I'll get you another."

"No, Eric. This whole thing was my fault. If I hadn't started yelling to get an echo, none of it would have happened."

"Don't be silly. You can't be sure you started the landslide." He tapped the end of her nose lightly.

Her cheeks flushed. She lowered her eyes.

"Well, let's get going," Eric said. "But if you start to feel even a little woozy, stop. You'll come up with me."

Jena nodded. Eric helped her into the saddle. Diablo, still ashamed, stood quietly. In a second Eric was up on Buckthorn. "Stay right behind me. We'll take it slow."

Chapter Eight

It was after five before they reached La Paloma. There wasn't a muscle in Jena's body that didn't ache. She could feel a swollen bruise on her hip, another on the back of her head.

Halfway through the journey, Jena had almost collapsed, and Eric had insisted she double up with him. "You're getting up with me before you fall off. I shouldn't have let you ride at all."

"It's all right," Jena had said wearily, "but I couldn't have gone much further."

When they started out again, Jena had leaned back against Eric and closed her eyes. Her brain felt fuzzy. But she knew that with Eric's chest pressed against her back, she felt very content.

"OK?" he had whispered.

"OK." Then they had both lapsed into silence

as the full impact of their near accident settled in.

At the sound of hoofbeats in the stable yard, Max came jogging out of his office. "Well, it's about time! I was just about to saddle up and go looking for you. Good heavens, Jena! What happened to you!" The frown that had been etched on his brow was rapidly replaced by anxiety as he saw the bruised and scratched girl.

"There was a landslide—in Lost Canyon," Jena managed to get out. "Diablo panicked and threw me. Eric got us out just in time."

Max swore under his breath. "Landslide! What started it going?"

"I did," Jena responded, "trying to get an echo."

Eric broke in. "It was probably ready to go, anyway." He helped Jena dismount, then reached out an arm to steady her.

"Bring her into the house," Max told him, "while I throw these horses in the corral."

Jena was grateful for Eric's support. As he helped her through the kitchen doorway, Maria looked up from the counter where she was preparing dinner, gasped, and dropped her knife so it went clattering onto the drainboard.

"Madre mía!"

Maria came running forward as Jena grimaced and took a seat in one of the kitchen chairs. "Ah, look at you, all blood and dirt."

She hurried back to the sink again, returning with a basin of soapy water and towels. Wringing one out, she pulled up a chair beside Jena and began washing her cuts. "What happened? The child looks as though she fell down a mountain. . . . No, you be still, Jena, while I clean these cuts. Eric can talk."

"Actually," Eric began, "the mountain almost fell down on her." He recounted the afternoon's events, while Maria shook her head and clucked her tongue from time to time and Jena gave out an "Ouch! That stings!" as Maria dabbed at her wounds. Eric was just about finished with his story when Max came running into the kitchen.

"How is she?"

"Nothing that a little rest and a long hot bath will not mend," Maria answered as she applied iodine to Jena's scratches. "Which is where I am going to take her right now."

"Not yet, Maria," Jena protested. "Let me sit for a minute. It feels so good." Actually the thought of the hot, soothing water on her sore muscles was enticing, too. She just didn't want to leave Eric. But when the men joined Maria in coaxing her upstairs, Jena let herself be persuaded, looking back quickly over her shoulder at Eric.

"Eric can sit here and talk with Max," Maria said firmly, "and later I will serve us all a good, hot supper."

Once in Jena's room, Maria helped Jena out

of her ragged clothes, exclaiming as she did, "Ah, the bruises all over your back."

"That's where I landed," Jena said, "on a bed of rocks."

"Sí, it is obvious."

As Jena eased down into the chin-deep suds, she sighed. She could almost feel the stiffness seeping out of her muscles. She lounged for half an hour, letting the heat soak into her, then, wanting to get back to Eric, she climbed out and dried herself. She dressed in the least confining clothing she could find—a lovely blue sundress that accentuated the color of her eyes, and a pair of thin-strapped sandals. Because her muscles were still sore, Maria helped her brush the tangles and brambles from her blond hair until it once again fell in a shining mass to below her shoulders. As she looked at herself in the mirror, Jena saw the sparkle in her eyes, the glow in her cheeks, and knew that despite the red slashes on her skin, she looked very pretty.

Eric, Max, and Pepe, who had since joined them, looked up as Jena returned to the kitchen.

"That's some transformation," Eric said, grinning as he stood to hold out the chair next to his. "What wonders a bath will do." Then more quietly, for her ears only, he said, "Feel all right? You had me worried."

"I feel good—a little sore, but OK."

Gently touching her shoulder in response, he sat down next to her.

As Maria brought the hot plates of food to the table, the conversation became brisk, almost gay, as though everyone wanted to forget the near tragedy of the afternoon. Jena wasn't thinking of the landslide anymore; she was thinking of Eric. Every time she glanced his way she felt heady and elated.

Eric was feeling carefree, too, more relaxed than he had felt in months. It was just the relief that it was over, he told himself, that Jena was all right.

"That was a nice piece of work you did today, Eric," Max was saying as he soaked the gravy off his plate with a crust of bread. "Real quick thinking. We owe you a lot of thanks, and if Jena's father was here, he'd say the same."

"I only did what any sane person would have done," Eric protested modestly. "Got the heck out as fast as we could."

"Still some mighty handy riding. I know that canyon, don't forget. You need a mountain goat under you to get out with any speed."

"Well, I had plenty of practice in tough situations at my father's ranch. I remember the time . . . I was about fourteen"—he fingered the salt-shaker, smiling as the memory came rushing back—"and there was this girl in my class, lived on the place next to ours, who I had the worst crush on. She was pretty, a big flirt, and had every guy in the class falling for her. I tried to talk to her a couple of times and got nowhere,

but there was a local rodeo, a calf-roping con-
test coming up, and I was determined to get
out there and impress her. Every afternoon after
my homework and chores, I was out in the
pasture on my horse, practicing. I thought I
had it licked. I was a pretty good rider and
roper, and I didn't think there was a guy around
who could beat me. Well, my father's ranch
hands were watching all of this. They knew
about Corinne and were having a pretty good
laugh at my expense—and thought they'd have
a little fun. The day of the rodeo came. I could
hardly sleep the night before. My number was
finally called, and I got out there in the ring,
cocky as could be. They let the calf out, and I
went flying after it, my rope in the air. It landed
around the calf's neck. My horse started back-
ing off to hold it tight, then funny things started
happening. I felt like I was wobbling, then my
saddle started sliding sideways. The next thing
I knew, I wasn't sitting on the horse but hanging *under* it, while he was still going backward
holding the rope taut. I remember seeing those
churning legs and thinking, this is it. Hold on
tight or you're mincemeat. Thank God the horse
had enough sense to know something was
wrong, and he stopped dead in his tracks. I
landed on my head in the dust. The audience
was roaring—you would have thought I was the
rodeo clown. Boy, was I mad! I had figured it
out by then and knew it was the ranch hands

who had loosened the cinch just before I rode out. I went storming out of the ring, looking like a complete fool. I found the bunch of them in back of the fence, holding their sides. My father was with them, laughing harder than the rest. 'I didn't know what they were up to,' he said to me, 'but I don't think I've ever seen anything funnier, son. And you needed some wind taken out of your sails. Girl's not worth it.'"

By the time Eric had finished, Max was slapping his thigh, chuckling away. "Wish I'd been there to see it! Pulled some pretty wild stunts in my day, but somehow you just don't seem the type, boy."

"No, you don't seem the type," Jena echoed. She couldn't seem to figure this guy out.

"A lot's happened since then." Eric looked sober but only momentarily. In a second he and Max looked at each other and burst into gales of laughter.

"Ah, and amigos," Pepe broke in, wiping the tears of laughter from his eyes, "I remember, too, these jokes. When I was just a boy in Mexico . . ."

And the stories went on, Max relating several. They all sat around the table until ten that night. Jena never thought of the passing hours, only realized that too soon they were gone when the kitchen clock chimed and Max pushed back his chair.

"Hate to break up this party, but I've got an early mornin' tomorrow. Eric, I'll give you a lift home, and you'll have to come by some Wednesday night for a game of cards at the bunkhouse . . . swap some more stories. Been a good evening."

"It has."

Everyone rose at once. Jena sent an anguished look in Eric's direction. There would be no private goodbyes . . . no chance for anything between them with everyone watching. She stood staring as everyone said good night, Max with his hand on Eric's shoulder in a friendly gesture, ushering him out the door. How could Max be so blind? How could he rush Eric out? Didn't he know that something had happened between Eric and her that day? And how could Eric walk out without saying, "Wait a minute, I have to talk to Jena." How?

Then in the doorway Eric turned. His eyes looked into hers. He smiled, a white flashing of his beautiful teeth. He winked. She winked back. Eric turned, and the men went out the door.

Jena, her head in the clouds, thought it would only be right to help Maria with the dishes that evening, but when Maria shooed her out the door to her room, she went. She had things to think about. Eric—and all the things that had happened that day, which she really hadn't had time to consider fully until now. She climbed the wrought-iron staircase to the upper story and went down the long balcony overlooking the courtyard to her room. There was a half-moon in the sky. The night had grown cool. She leaned over the railing and looked into the courtyard. The dim moonlight glinting off the fishpond gave the courtyard a fairy-tale quality. What was Eric thinking now? Jena wondered. Was he thinking about her? And what was this throbbing inside herself, this desire to be with him, listen to his voice, and just look at him?

It was a good feeling, yet scary, too. Did he feel the same? He had kissed her—but maybe he had only done that out of relief that she hadn't been buried under a landslide. She'd had so little experience with boys.

Still, he had winked at her as he had left the kitchen. Jena went to bed with that thought and had very happy dreams.

Chapter Nine

Max dropped Eric off at the gates of Del Costa, gave a friendly wave, and called out the window of the station wagon, "Come back, like I said. You'll be welcome."

"I will," Eric called back. The station wagon turned, and Eric treaded his way up the lamplit drive toward the modern beach cottage.

After stripping off his borrowed boots and socks inside the front door, Eric went straight to the stereo. He put on some mellow music, then went out on the deck. The moon cast its shadows and light over the waters, accenting the waves, giving a greenish tint to their crests.

He leaned his elbows on the rail and thrust his chin into his hands. What was he doing? This girl . . . Jena. What was she doing to him? It was getting out of proportion. He'd known from the beginning that she had something special—the way she had ridden that horse right up to him that first day on the beach, the way she had smiled. And today she had shown courage. He thought of how he had felt when she was thrown onto that pile of rocks, her golden hair spread all around her, tangled in the brush. He could pretend to himself that Eric Clayton had come down here for the summer to escape and that he wasn't going to get involved. Yet he knew in his heart it wasn't so. This Jena . . . Goldilocks . . . was something else.

He had liked their kiss—more than he had liked any of the sophisticated interludes he'd experienced since he'd gotten into the music business. Yet she was so innocent, so sweet and searching. He couldn't deceive her and put her on as he had done to some of the girls he'd met on the rock circuit. That world seemed far behind him now, a different universe. How was it possible that he'd been caught up so quickly in this relaxed ranch life-style? Maybe it was because his roots were in ranching and these last few days brought back memories.

But this vacation was only temporary, and he'd have to keep reminding himself of that fact. If he was the decent guy he had always considered himself to be, he would sit down and tell Jena the truth about himself—who he really was, where he really was going. Yet, if he did, it would change everything. She wouldn't see him in the same light. She might not be able to see the real person underneath the rock image. Selfishly he knew he didn't want it to end—not yet. Soon enough he'd have to return to his career.

Sighing, Eric crossed the patio and went into the house. He wouldn't find any solutions tonight. He was too confused and torn by conflicting emotions.

In the morning, as the housekeeper brought him his breakfast on the deck, he debated whether to go down to the beach again. With her bruises from the day before, Jena probably wouldn't come. Maybe he should call her and see how she was feeling. It was the least he could do. But, no, then he would be encouraging things. She'd think he wanted to see her again. He *did* want to see her again. But it was crazy. Back and forth he argued with himself. Finally his need to hear her voice won out. He'd just call, ask how she was . . . that was all.

Maria answered and put Jena right on.

"Jena?"

"Hi, Eric." Her voice was breathless, happy.

"Just called to see how you were."

"I'm fine. I feel great. Not even that sore. How about you? You walking bowlegged?"

He had to smile. "A little. Haven't gotten to the point of crutches yet."

"What are you up to?"

"Just finished my breakfast. What about you?"

"Oh, I don't know. Thought I might go out and see the filly. It's such a beautiful day!"

She sounded so cheerful, warm. Eric didn't know what came over him, but suddenly the words were out of his mouth. "I heard about some mission ruins up in the foothills. Want to take a look at them with me?"

"Sure, I'd love to."

"I'll come over and pick you up. Half an hour OK?"

"Fine. I'll be ready."

"See you then." Eric hung up and shook his head. What was the matter with him? He was acting completely on impulse—totally the opposite of what he'd set out to do. And then there was the small matter of his car. He hadn't thought about that when he had told her he'd pick her up, but how in heck was he going to explain a supposedly middle-class college kid owning a Ferrari? He could say he'd won it. That was a joke. Better yet he could say someone had asked him to take care of the car for the summer. Believable? Well, it was the best he could come up with.

He sighed heavily. This deceit. The lies were getting bigger and bigger.

When he picked Jena up and walked her to the car, her reaction was just what he had expected. She lifted her brows, giving him a sly glance.

"Nice, really nice! One of my father's friends had a car just like this, and it was always my dream to get to ride in it—better yet, drive it! A Ferrari, right? Where'd you get it?"

He was almost amazed when she seemed to swallow his story without question, then climbed in and exclaimed that this was going to be fun.

As they drove away from the ranch toward the mountains, the Ferrari clung to the winding road. Though he was tempted, Eric didn't dare push it too fast over the rough terrain; still they flew.

It was a beautiful, clear day without a touch of summer haze, and they enjoyed the ride to the mission. As they wandered among the ruins, both Jena and Eric felt a sense of serenity. It was as though the Spanish monks had left behind an ongoing peace in the adobe walls and archways. At first Eric and Jena walked side by side, Eric pointing out bits of mosaic, the remains of what must have been a grape arbor, a crumbled cistern. Then as they scaled the hillside behind for a better view, Eric took Jena's hand and continued holding it. They found a rocky ledge where they could sit and look down at the ruins and valley beyond. Jena cast a shy glance at Eric's profile. He was staring out at the view, where the town of Mission Valley was just a miniature landscape in the distance. He seemed deep in thought, far away. She wondered what he was thinking, if he was feeling the same fluttery contentment that she was. He had been especially quiet this morning during the ride and their walk. She wished she could look behind that handsome profile. There were so many things she wanted to know about him. But he seemed so reserved, she was afraid to ask.

At last Eric turned to see her watching and smiled.

"Nice, isn't it?"

Jena nodded.

"Wonder what the Spaniards saw when they first came here—if it looks much different now."

He wasn't really looking for an answer, and Jena gave him none.

"Must have been a lonely life, though. No cities to visit. Just the mountains and the ocean and the sky." He picked a pebble off the ground with his free hand and toyed with it. He looked almost wistful. "Simple life—no distractions."

"Wouldn't you get bored?"

He threw the pebble in the air and caught it, still staring out into the distance. "Yeah, you're right. I guess I would." He dropped the pebble, then dusted his hand on his jeans impatiently, as though he'd just had an unpleasant thought.

Before Jena had a chance to say anything else, he rose quickly, pulling her with him. "Let's walk down the other way."

As he turned, their eyes met and held. His expression was serious, almost troubled. Jena felt instinctively drawn to him, ready to reach up a hand and touch his cheek. Then suddenly the spell was broken as he looked away and led her down the trail.

Eric stayed for lunch at La Paloma. He felt powerless, as though caught in some strange whirlwind. His mind told him what he should be doing, yet he was behaving exactly the opposite. The people at the ranch were already treating him like an old friend, not only grateful for what he'd done for Jena the previous day but also seeming to genuinely like him. He felt at home, comfortable. He realized he could easily have spent the rest of the day at the ranch and have enjoyed it, but he knew it was important to put some space between himself and Jena, to be alone for a while and think. He smiled ruefully to himself as he put his car in gear and roared out of the drive. At least his willpower, little that he seemed to have lately, was good for something.

Chapter Ten

Yet despite what his head told him, Eric became a regular visitor to La Paloma. He pushed his doubts and guilt to the back of his mind, taking each day as it came.

Jena had called him to ask if he wanted to join her for a few sets of tennis, and that had been all the temptation he'd needed. There followed days of morning and afternoon rides across the ranch land, galloping along the wet sand beside the pounding surf. They frolicked with the filly. Jena took him on a tour of the house. Eric drove her to La Jolla for a shopping spree. In doing this he realized he was growing careless with his cover. Although Jena had no idea of his real identity, they easily could have run into a number of people in the bustling, picturesque resort town who might have recognized him. He was taking a big chance, but somehow his desire to do something fun with Jena—see her eyes light up and hear her tinkling laughter—was more important at the moment. He pushed all fears of being found out to the back of his mind. He deceived himself into believing that if he ignored the problem, it would go away.

His growing feelings for her were something else he refused to think about or define. As long as he kept it light, he convinced himself, just friendly, just good companions doing the things they liked to do together, everything would be all right. There would be no broken hearts when he left for L.A. in a few weeks. The problem was that he was finding it harder and harder not to reach out and take her hand, touch her, put his arm around her shoulder. He couldn't keep his eyes off her or stop thinking of her nearly every hour of his waking day.

They spent many hours talking together as Eric told her more of his days in Wyoming, his years of growing up, and she told him of New York, Chase Girls' School, vacationing with her parents, the places she had traveled to. They compared notes on what it had been like growing up in their different backgrounds, but while Jena was willing, even anxious, to talk of her future plans, Eric never talked beyond the past.

Jena thought it strange that he said nothing to her of his days at Berkeley, his plans after graduation. Did he have many friends? What were his hobbies? He had said he liked music once when she'd asked, but that was all. If she tried to press him for answers, he frowned and changed the subject, so she stopped pressing. But why had he come down here all by himself? There had to be more to it than the fact he was house-sitting at Del Costa. His family was far from poor, and Eric didn't have to house-sit just to put a roof over his head. Why cut himself off? She couldn't understand why he would voluntarily come to an isolated beach house, far from his friends and the world in general. It wasn't something she would have done, but then, she had been looking for something just the opposite this summer—excitement, contact with the world outside the protected environment of a girls' school—and she had found it. But still, Jena felt frustrated. Eric left so many questions unanswered. They had gotten to be good friends, but Jena often felt a wall between them. It couldn't really be because he was a few years older, could it? And she was disappointed that the promise of romance, the kiss after the landslide, seemed to have been left behind in the Lost Canyon rubble.

Jena still had high hopes, though, and she had found a friend in Susan Strasberg, too, who had called several times since their first meeting. The summer really was turning out to be wonderful—far beyond her expectations—and she was grinning when she met Susan for tennis.

Susan came running over as she saw Jena approaching the courts. "How are you?"

"Great. How are you?"

"Can't complain. I'm really beginning to enjoy myself down here." The two girls found an empty court and began unzipping their racket covers. "So what's been happening with you since last time?"

"A lot." Jena giggled, unable to keep her happiness from lighting up her face. "I didn't say anything before, but I met this guy, Susan—"

"And you didn't tell me!"

"I was afraid to get my hopes up too high. I met him on the beach at La Paloma." Jena went on to describe their meeting, his saving her from the landslide, the times they had been together since. "He's just the greatest, Susan. I can't believe it!"

"What's he look like? Where's he from? What's his name?"

"Wait a minute, Susan," Jena protested, laughing. "Give me a break. I'll tell you everything. He's tall, brown hair and eyes—nice looking with the cutest dimple in his chin, and he's terrific. His name is Eric, and he goes to Berkeley. He's spending the summer at the house up the beach from the ranch—and we've seen each other almost every day since we met!"

"That's wonderful! I'm really happy, and you'll never guess. I met a boy, too!"

"Did you? Where?"

"Here at the club. I came down alone Saturday to use the pool, and he was there by himself. We started talking. His family has a ranch nearby."

"I didn't know there were any interesting guys in the neighborhood," Jena said. "What's his name?"

"Willie . . . Willie Jenkins."

"Willie Jenkins!" Jena's eyes popped.

"You know him?"

"I haven't seen him in a couple of years, but, yeah, I sure do."

"Isn't he fantastic? And he's so blond and he's got the most wonderful blue eyes. He's so interesting—he was telling me all about the area, and he asked me to go to a movie with him this weekend."

Jena swallowed. She didn't dare tell Susan, who seemed so delighted, what her impressions of Willie Jenkins had always been. And the guy Susan was describing sounded very little like the Willie Jena remembered—a dull, slightly overweight kid with a bad complexion. The only similarities were the blond hair and blue eyes. Could they be talking about the same person? But, then, it had been two years, and Jena realized she had changed a lot in that time, too.

"He starts college this fall," Susan was saying, "in San Diego, so he won't even be that far away, and he's going out for football. He did so well in his senior year in high school, he expects to make first string—not that he bragged about it or anything. I practically had to pull the information out of him."

"Really." All Jena could think of was the braggart Willie had once been. Well, people change.

"I wish you could meet him," Susan exclaimed. "Oh, but you already know him."

"And tell him I said hello. I think he'll remember me." She grinned.

"Sure will. But when am I going to get to meet this Eric of yours?"

"There's a square dance Max told me about in a couple of weeks. Maybe we could all get together."

"Sounds like a good idea! And I'm really glad about your news. You seem so happy."

"I am." Jena smiled with conviction.

Yet as the days passed, the questions in Jena's mind really began tormenting her. It was wonderful seeing Eric, being with him, but she still didn't fully understand him. He seemed to be holding himself in check, just as she would hold Diablo if they were roaring down a steep mountain valley. Jena knew she was beginning to care very much and that it was a new and different feeling from any she had experienced in the past. It was heady, overwhelming—the kind of thing she had dreamed would happen to her one day. But what did he think? What did he feel? Was the fact that he spent so much time with her an indication that he liked her? Yes, he did like her—that was obvious—but was it only as a friend, or was it something more? He hadn't once tried to kiss her again, and that bothered her.

She saw his face in her dreams every night—his profile, his warm brown eyes, the way his lips moved when he talked. It was almost like a Grecian statue coming to life. In the mornings when she brushed her hair before the mirror, she wondered how Eric would feel about this hairdo, or that; if he would like the outfit she had on; or if she should change her blouse. . . . Standing before her mirror, she would analyze herself, her features, her long blond hair, her figure, and the fit of her clothes. She had never had any reason to feel unhappy with her appearance. She wasn't unhappy with it now, but what did Eric think? He never said much, only looked at her and smiled. He complimented her on her riding, on a good backhand in tennis, laughed when she told a joke, was intrigued when she discussed history, her favorite subject, but still he remained a mystery.

Chapter Eleven

Jena, Eric, and Max rode together to the Saturday night square dance at El Pino. Susan and Willie had planned on meeting them there, but the day before Susan had come down with a sore throat and fever, and her mother had made her stay home. Just the same, it turned out to be a hilariously good evening. All the ranchers and townspeople within a twenty-mile radius had shown up, eager for some good old-fashioned fun. Although both Eric and Jena had known the steps and calls years before, neither had had much practice lately. They spent a few hours the two days before the dance brushing up with Hank, one of the ranch hands, who gave them pointers, but even so it was a comedy of errors as they bumbled their way through the dances, laughing uproariously at their mistakes.

"That was my foot," Eric said once to Jena through gritted teeth as they swung through a reel.

"Just getting you back," she said, grinning, "for that do-si-do when you nearly knocked me on the floor."

"Well, if you'd been where you were supposed to be—" he began, then burst out laughing at the expression on her face.

But by the time the band stopped for their first break, Eric and Jena were both getting the knack of it again. Max came over as they were standing by the refreshment table drinking lemonade.

"Enjoying yourselves? Nice crowd. Haven't seen a turnout like this for a couple of years."

"It's great," Jena answered, then cast a sly look at Max. "I notice you're having a pretty good time yourself. Who's the lady?"

"Lady?" Max's tanned, ruddy skin flushed. "What lady?"

"Don't play dumb, Max. You've danced practically every dance with her. Nice-looking lady with dark auburn curls."

"Oh, that's just Myra Lloyd—known her for years," Max said self-consciously. "She's been kinda lonely since her husband passed on a year or so back. Felt sorry for her and asked her to dance—nothin' else."

"Mmmm," Jena said wisely.

"Don't tease the poor guy now, Jena," Eric remarked, but he was smiling widely. "Looks like a nice woman, Max, and she certainly seems to be enjoying your company. She's looking for you now, as a matter of fact." Eric motioned with his head toward the other side of the room.

Jena had never seen self-assured Max look so flustered. She hid her smile behind her hand.

"Ah, well, yeah, I did say I'd bring her a cold drink. If you kids will excuse me." Max hurried away as if there were a swarm of bees on his tail. As soon as he was out of hearing distance, Eric and Jena broke into laughter.

"I never thought I'd see ol' Max get caught," Jena said.

"What makes you think he's caught? He's probably just having a good time. And he's not all that old, Jena—only in his forties."

"Guess he seems old to me because I've known him since I was a baby, and I've never seen him pay that much attention to one woman. He usually mixes around." She was thoughtful for a moment. "But I guess it must get lonely for him being at the ranch all the time with no one but the hands for company."

"What are you cooking up in that little head of yours?"

"Oh, nothing—just thinking of the possibilities."

"It doesn't pay to meddle, Jena."

"I know . . . I know."

"Come on." Eric put down his empty glass. "The band's starting again."

"Let's sit this one out. I want to rest a little more, and maybe I can pick up a few hints by watching the others."

"Yeah." He chuckled. "We need all the help we can get."

As Jena watched the dancers, Eric's eyes were drawn to the band. He didn't do it consciously, but it was part of his musician's instinct to listen to another musician's performance. There was a fiddler, a foot-tapping older man who really put his heart into it, two guitarists, one of whom was also calling the steps, and an accordion player.

"That fiddler's pretty good," Eric said to Jena after listening for a few minutes. "Reminds me of how my uncle used to play."

"I didn't know you knew anything about fiddling."

"When I was a kid, my uncle taught me a little. Then I switched over to guitar."

"You play the guitar?"

"Mmmm." Eric was still listening and answered without thinking.

"Are you good?"

"Pretty good, I guess."

"Well, why don't you get up and play? People are always coming up from the floor to play and sing. It's part of the fun." She took Eric's arm.

"We can ask the caller. Maybe after this next number—"

"Whoa!" Eric suddenly realized the potential hot spot his thoughtless words were leading him into. That was all he needed to do—get up on the floor and advertise himself. He was lucky that most of the people at the dance were past the age of rock madness and that no one had recognized him. He held back as Jena pulled forward. "Listen, all I ever did was fool around a little. I'm not getting up on that stage."

"It's just for fun, Eric. No one here's a professional."

"Absolutely not!"

Jena would have continued prodding Eric, but she took one look at his grim face and realized he was deadly serious. "Oh, all right. I won't push you. But will you play for me sometime? We have a beautiful Spanish guitar at La Paloma."

"I'll think about it." Eric relaxed. "Let's dance. I think I can handle this one without falling all over my feet."

Toward the end of the evening the band slowed the tempo to some traditional waltzes. As Eric took Jena out onto the floor, he smiled down at her. "Now at least I'll know what I'm doing." Then he pulled her close, and Jena felt warm and tingling all over. Her head spun with the firm pressure of his body, the clean scent of his cologne.

"You smell good," she whispered.

"So do you . . . almost edible." His lips brushed against her hair, and an involuntary shiver went down her spine.

"I like these dances much better, Goldilocks." His hand squeezed hers. "For obvious reasons."

"You're a very good dancer."

He chuckled. "Flattery will get you everywhere, as much as I know you're putting me on."

"No, it's true. You're the best I've ever danced with."

"And how many boys have you danced with?"

"Well . . . only a few."

"That's what I thought."

"But I'd rather dance with you than anyone else."

Eric didn't say anything for a moment, then dropped his cheek closer against her hair. His voice was quiet. "The feeling's mutual, Goldilocks." And Jena sighed, closed her eyes, and let the music and the sensation of dancing with Eric carry her away until the chords of "Goodnight, Sweetheart" signaled everyone it was time to go.

Eric rode back with Max and Jena in the station wagon to La Paloma, where he had left his car. They were all in happy spirits as they recounted the events of the evening.

Jena couldn't resist teasing Max a little more. "Why didn't you offer Mrs. Lloyd a ride home? Eric and I wouldn't have minded."

For a change Max didn't prevaricate. "She had her own wheels. Supposed to stop by tomorrow night and take her to a movie."

"Ohee!" Jena cried. "Things are getting interesting!"

"Now you hold on there, missy. You ain't so big I can't still take a hand to your bottom." But his lips twitched in a grin.

"Seriously, Max, I think it's great."

"No use countin' chickens before they're hatched."

"But it doesn't hurt to count the eggs . . . just in case."

Max gave her a playful tap, then joined in their laughter. When they arrived at La Paloma, Eric declined an invitation to come in for a snack.

"It's getting late, Jena. You need your sleep—so do I, for that matter. Walk me to my car."

Jena willingly complied.

"I'll see you guys tomorrow," Max called out, heading for his cottage.

"Good night, Max."

It was a beautifully clear night, and the moonlight was slipping through the eucalyptus branches to dapple the driveway.

"I had a good time tonight, Jena." Eric paused by the door of his car.

"So did I."

"See you tomorrow?"

She nodded.

He took both her hands and held them for a moment as he looked down at her face. Her golden hair touched by the moonlight hung like a pale halo around her shoulders.

"Well, good night, Goldilocks. Sweet dreams." There was just the tiniest pressure of his fingers against hers. Then he climbed quickly into the car and started the engine.

Jena watched as the Ferrari disappeared down the drive. Her eyes were misty with disappointment. She thought for sure that tonight of all nights he was going to kiss her. It had been a wonderful evening, and she knew he had enjoyed it as much as she had. While they were dancing, she had sensed a feeling in him—something more than friendship, something close to the heady happiness she was feeling herself. But nothing had happened. What was she doing wrong? Why couldn't he care as much about her as she cared for him?

A few nights later Eric invited her out to dinner to a good restaurant in La Jolla. It was going to be a special evening, he said. Jena was thrilled. She dressed with care that night in her prettiest dress, a soft, flowing blue print that she and her mother had purchased in New York a few months before. With her thin-strapped heels and her hair in french braids, Jena knew she looked her best. She was sure of it as she came down the staircase and saw the appreciative gleam in Eric's eyes. "You look beautiful, Goldilocks."

And he looked so handsome, Jena felt her breath catch in her throat. She had never seen him dressed up before, and the light summer jacket looked fantastic on him, emphasizing the width of his shoulders and the deep tan of his face. He looked older, too, more sophisticated.

They dined in a small, candle-lit restaurant perched on a cliff over the bay. From the open terrace they had a sweeping view of the hills to either side and the Pacific. That night Eric showed Jena a side of himself she had never seen, a cosmopolitan flare that astounded her. He ordered from the menu with the same careless skill her father would have shown—the ease of someone who had been around and was used to expensive restaurants. He was the perfect gentleman—not that she'd ever found anything to fault in his manners—holding the chair for her, making sure her dinner was exactly what she wanted, putting her at ease with his own comfortable conversation.

When they left the restaurant, they strolled along the cliff path for a while, leaning on the railings, listening to the waves crashing and lapping below.

"When do you have to go back to New York?" Eric asked unexpectedly.

Jena looked at him sharply. "Not for over another month."

Eric nodded. He obviously had something on his mind.

"Why do you ask?"

"I don't know. The last few weeks just seem to have gone by so fast."

"They always do when you're having a good time. How about you? You have another month, too."

"I was hoping on that. We'll see. . . ." He was looking out over the water. "What are you going to do when you go back East?"

"Go to school, of course. What else is there?"

"No, I mean in your free time. What do you do for fun?"

"If my parents are home, I spend the weekends with them in the City. Otherwise, I hang around my room, maybe go to the movies with some of the girls. There's not an awful lot to do at Chase." A small, puzzled frown appeared on Jena's brow. "Is there something wrong?"

"No, I was just wondering."

"You'll be doing the same sort of thing, I imagine, though you have more freedom at college than I have."

He nodded again, stared ahead silently, then shrugged his broad shoulders and straightened up. He took Jena's hand. "We'll drive back along the coast. It's a perfect night for it."

But that night, too, he left Jena at her door with a chaste squeezing of hands and a "Sweet dreams, Goldilocks," and Jena laid in her bed for a long time, staring at the ceiling and wondering what was going on. What was in his mind and heart? His intent glances, the warm tone of his voice told her he cared, yet he never stepped beyond the bounds of friendship.

Chapter Twelve

Five weeks had passed since the day of their meeting on the beach. But Eric deliberately refused to count the days, just as he refused to let himself look at his feelings too deeply. He congratulated himself for keeping his relationship with Jena on strictly a friendly basis. He had done what he had set out to do—enjoy the summer and her company with no ties and no hurt feelings. So what if he couldn't stop thinking of her, if she was in his dreams every night, if it was taking every ounce of his willpower to continue to keep things cool, to not reach out for her, hold her, kiss her? By ignoring his doubts, he kept them at arm's length. If he took each day as it came, he didn't have to think about where it was heading.

That day Eric and Jena had planned a picnic on the beach. They packed a lunch and everything else they would need in their saddlebags and rode out from the ranch just after noon. There was a trickling stream just behind the beach, where they unsaddled the horses and let them graze on the sparse grass. Gathering what they needed from the saddlebags, they walked out across the sand. The Pacific was a brilliant, deep blue, sparkling in the sunlight; its rushing waves looked cool and refreshing. After spreading and anchoring the blanket and stripping down to their suits, Eric called out. "Race you to the water!"

"You know you'll beat me," Jena said, laughing. "Your legs are longer than mine."

But still she came in a close second as they plunged, still running, into the rollers, dove beneath the waves, both laughing when their heads broke above the surface again.

"This wakes you up real quick." Eric grinned. "Not as warm as it looks. Swim with me awhile."

Jena agreed and started a graceful crawl beside Eric, parallel to the beach. They swam a hundred yards, rested, and turned back. When Jena reached their starting point, paused to tread water and look around, there was no sign of Eric. For a moment she panicked, but she knew he was a good swimmer. Nothing could have happened to him. She turned to scan the area behind her more closely, when suddenly arms reached from beneath and pulled her under. The saltwater stinging her open eyes, she saw Eric's face close beside her, his cheeks dimpled, his raised brows silently asking, "Scared you, didn't I?"

She reached out a hand, gave his ribs a good tickle, then surged to the surface again. His head popped up next to hers a second later, his mouth spitting a stream of water.

"You made me laugh under there, you minx, and I got a mouthful."

"Serves you right," she said, giggling. "Two can play the game."

"Ready to swim in?"

Nodding her head, Jena started for the shore, letting her body ride with the incoming waves, then scrambling onto the beach out of the undertow.

Eric plopped down next to her on the blanket. The sun felt warm and tingling on their wet bodies. He reached out and took her hand, then they both closed their eyes and let the sun lull them into a doze.

Jena roused first, rolling over onto her back. Eric's eyes were still closed; he seemed asleep. Her lids drifted shut as the sun bathed her face. When she opened them a little later, Eric's eyes were open, intently watching her. There was a softness in the brown depths she had never seen before. He moved to his side, resting his head on his arm, still gazing at her.

"I fell asleep." His voice was foggy.

She smiled.

"Had a nice dream, too."

"Did you?" she said quietly. "What about?"

"Can't tell you that . . . but it was good."

Something in the tone of his voice made her blush. "We should check the horses."

"Mmmm." It was a lazy sound, and he didn't seem inclined to move.

"If they wander off, we'll have a hard time catching them."

"Suppose you're right, but I don't feel like moving—at least not to check the horses."

"You stay, then." She smiled. "I can run over." She sat up and reached for her sandals.

He sat up quickly, too. "I'll go with you. I don't want you out—" He changed his mind. "In case there's a problem."

He took her hand as they walked. Jena's heart was beating unnaturally. Was it just his mood? There was something underlying his words and soft looks—was it what she had been waiting for?

"The horses should stay pretty close to where we left them," Eric said easily as they walked across the sand. "The only decent grass and shade are over there."

Diablo looked up and nickered when he saw them approaching. Buckthorn was right beside him, and the two had been lazing in the shade of a tree. Neither animal seemed inclined to wander.

"Well, you were right," Jena told Eric. "Still I feel better that we checked."

"Better safe than sorry."

They patted the horses' necks, then headed back toward the blanket. Warm and sticky again from the exercise and hot sun, they dove back into the waves, swam some more, then went back to the blanket for a cold drink. Jena pulled out a deck of cards, and they played a game of rummy, anchoring the cards with pebbles to keep the wind from whipping them away.

"Hungry yet?" she asked when the game was over.

"A little. My appetite isn't what it usually is, but bring out some of those sandwiches."

"What do you want? Turkey or tuna?"

"Turkey."

She handed him one. "Coke?"

"OK."

"Maria made some homemade chocolate chip cookies, too."

"Those I can always find room for."

They ate in silence, though Jena couldn't help noticing the gentle looks he continued to give her. This time she smiled.

As she packed the food away, Eric leaned back on his elbows and looked toward the crashing waves. "You know this is one of the most perfect spots on the whole coast."

"I've always thought so—especially this summer," she added a little shyly.

"Why this summer?" He looked at her out of the corner of his eyes.

"Because it's nice when there's someone to talk to, to do things with."

Eric reached for her hand and absentmindedly rubbed her fingers. "You're right." His voice was so quiet she barely heard it.

When he turned away, Jena studied his face, felt that familiar fluttering in her stomach, was extremely conscious of the warm pressure of his fingers on hers.

They sat for a long time, listening to the waves, the rush of the wind, the cry of the gulls, the peacefulness.

Eric suddenly jumped up. "What do you say? Another swim before it gets too chilly?"

Jena was ready. She leaped to her feet and dashed beside him into the water. They stayed in longer this time, swimming, splashing, and diving like a pair of dolphins, catching hold of each other's feet beneath the water, sabotaging each other with surprise attacks. When they finally climbed out, dripping and exhausted, the sun was dipping low, and there was the first hint of evening chill in the air.

"Got any matches?" Eric asked as they grabbed their towels to dry off.

"I probably do. Max always packs an emergency

survival kit in my saddlebag." Jena laughed. "Why?"

"I thought we could start a fire and warm up before we got back. There's plenty of driftwood on the beach."

"Hey, that's a great idea! We can watch the sunset."

"Dig out a hollow in the sand, and I'll get some wood," Eric instructed, striding off to above the high-water mark. He returned with several armloads as Jena prepared the bed of the fire, crumpling the scrap papers from their lunch in the bottom to get the wood started. She found a box of matches and handed them to Eric after he had made a careful pile of small bits of driftwood. The kindling, dry from the sun, caught quickly. Eric gradually piled on larger pieces until he had a warm and glowing fire.

"Perfect." He stood back to admire his handiwork, then pulled the blanket closer behind the fire and motioned to Jena. "Come on and get warm. You look like you're freezing."

Jena couldn't argue with that. The wind was chilly, and her still-wet suit didn't help. She sat down next to Eric and stretched out her hands to the flames. He wrapped his arm around her shoulders, and she snuggled closer for warmth.

The sky over the ocean turned a beautiful crimson color as they watched the slowly sinking sun. They were both more comfortable now as their suits dried and their bodies heated.

Jena dropped her head onto Eric's shoulder. She felt contented, relaxed, pleasantly tired from all the exercise, sun, and salt air.

"It's been a good day," Eric said softly, his breath whispering through her hair.

"It has." She sighed. "I wish it didn't have to end."

"I guess we should get back pretty soon before they start to worry about you."

"They won't. Max and Maria trust you. Let's wait until the sun's all the way down."

"Whatever you say, Goldilocks. I'm not in any hurry to leave, anyway." He tweaked her nose teasingly.

Jena turned her head and looked up at his face.

Eric felt a thrill go through him as her beautiful blue eyes caught his. He felt himself drowning. Her lips were so close; she smelled fresh and sweet from the salt and the sun. He couldn't fight it. All day he had been waging a losing battle with his feelings, and he couldn't pretend any longer that Jena was just another friend.

Slowly he lifted his hand to gently touch her cheek, to rub his thumb over the softness of her lips. "Oh, Jena." He sighed. Then his mouth found hers. It was a light, gentle kiss that became more passionate as he sensed an answering response from her. He wasn't thinking anymore. It was as though a dam had broken to let his feelings flow freely, at last without restraint.

He felt Jena's arms circle his neck as she melted closer against him. He kissed her again and again; her lips, her cheeks, her nose, her closed eyes. When he finally lifted his head, it was only to whisper in a breathless voice, "Jena, I care about you so much . . . I really do."

At his words Jena's heart was flying, soaring as though it were no longer part of her body. This was what she had been waiting for. This was what she had wanted to happen so badly. Eric cared about her. Eric! It couldn't be true . . . yet it was.

"Jena," he whispered, his lips against her ear. "Jena, did you hear me?"

"Yes."

"How do you feel?"

"I feel the same." She pulled a little away so she could look at him.

"I was afraid to tell you," he said. "Afraid to admit it to myself."

"Why?"

"Because . . . because I was afraid it wouldn't last . . . that it was just a summer thing."

"It doesn't have to be."

Eric didn't answer. He didn't know what to say. He had admitted his feelings to himself and to her, and for the moment he couldn't think any further.

And Jena couldn't ask for any more, not yet.

She was still whirling from the fact he cared. Now all his past actions seemed to make sense—his aloofness, his holding back after the time of their first kiss. She wouldn't have wanted it any other way, though, because now when he stated his feelings, she could believe him. It wasn't a spur of the moment thing.

Eric watched her face as these thoughts flitted across her mind. He suddenly felt so alive, so free, so human, but also so vulnerable. And he knew now he had been asking the impossible of himself when he had expected to remain uninvolved in his relationship with Jena. From the first moment he had seen her, he had known where it could lead . . . where it could end. But he didn't want to think of endings . . . not here . . . not today.

He pulled her close again, against the warmth of his chest. He ran his fingers through her thick, glossy, golden hair. The flames of the fire licked upward toward a sky spattered with russet, crimson, and pink. He found her lips again, sealing their new-found feelings the only way he knew how at the moment. As they clung to each other tightly, Eric felt his senses whirling, carrying him away. It was so good to hold her in his arms.

With the touch of his lips, the gentle warmth of his arms, Jena thought she could never experience anything so perfect or wonderful again. Eric's kisses brought a feeling better than any she had imagined in her dreams. She didn't want it to end; she didn't want this day to be over or darkness to come. Was this what loving a boy was like? This incredible all-consuming sensation that threatened to sweep her into the air?

She was only semiconscious of his actions as he pressed his body more tightly toward her. She only half-heard the heaviness of his breathing. But then his hands started to drift with gentle insistence.

Eric felt Jena freeze, start to pull away. He froze himself. It took him a moment to clear his brain and leash his emotions. He hadn't meant to get carried away. This was a girl he not only cared about but respected.

"Eric, I think we're going too far," Jena whispered.

"I know. I'm sorry."

"It's all right."

"I wasn't trying to push you."

"I know."

"It's just that I care so much."

"So do I, Eric. I'm—I'm just not ready."

"That's OK. I was going too fast." His voice still wasn't fully steady.

"I love you, Eric."

"And I love you, Goldilocks." He leaned away from her, brushing the hair from her face. "We'd better go back."

Jena nodded.

"I meant everything I said today."

"I know."

He helped her to her feet. "We'll have to make sure this fire is out."

Jena, anxious for some activity to bring her down to earth, helped him to bury the fire under a pile of sand so that not one glowing ember could be seen. Together they collected the picnic things and rolled up the blanket. Their backs to each other, they pulled their jeans and shirts on over their bathing suits; both suddenly, inexplicably self-conscious. Each grabbing an armful of gear, they started toward the horses.

"We'll be lucky to get back while we can still see where we're going," Eric remarked as they saddled up.

"I know most of the trails by heart." Jena tightened Diablo's cinch and dropped the stirrup leather. She filled the saddlebags, then turned to see if Eric was ready.

He walked around Buckthorn's head and suddenly reached for Jena. They held each other tightly, silently. Without another word they mounted up and headed to La Paloma.

Chapter Thirteen

Eric was at La Paloma early the next morning. He had done a lot of thinking the night before. He realized only too well how much he'd been hiding from the truth. His feelings for Jena were real and had been growing for weeks. He knew he would have to talk to her soon— somehow find a way to explain who he really was and why he had deceived her for so long. He had plotted out all kinds of words in his head, discarded them, come up with new ones. Finally he decided that when the time came, he would just tell the truth as best he could and hope that she would accept his reasons and understand why it had taken him so long to tell her. If they were going to continue from where they were now—and he wanted them to—Jena had to know who he was.

Why had it taken him so long? Why had he kept putting it off? He cursed himself. Had he ruined everything by waiting until the last moment? He was going to change things now . . . as soon as he had a chance to say it all. He was nervous, afraid. Yet if everything fell apart, he had only himself to blame.

As he pulled his car into the drive and parked, Max came out of his office to investigate and pointed Eric in the direction of the stables. He walked up behind Jena as she was leaning over the stall, coaxing the filly toward the apple she held in her hand. Eric gripped Jena around the waist and dropped a warm kiss on the back of her neck.

At first she jumped, but when she felt his lips, she turned quickly. "Someday someone will teach you not to sneak up on people."

"And how will they do that?" He grinned.

"Should I show you?"

"I'd love it—I think."

"You will." And she kissed him, not just a peck, but with feeling.

"Mmmm."

"Have you learned your lesson?"

"I was thinking about you last night."

"I was thinking about you, too."

"Jena, we have to talk—"

But she interrupted him. "I'm full of energy this morning. I feel so happy! Let's go play some tennis. The courts should be free this early."

"I'm not dressed." He motioned to his jeans.

"We'll stop by your place on the way, and you can change."

He was swept up by her exuberant spirits. "OK. I'll talk to Max while you change." He realized she wasn't in any mood for a serious discussion. He wished he could have been so carefree.

As they drove to his place, Jena was bubbling. Once she stopped to look over at his serious face. She immediately sobered.

"Is something wrong, Eric? What is it?"

This wasn't the right time to bring it up either, he thought. He'd tell her later, after they had played and he could drive her up into the mountains. "Oh, nothing." He shrugged and forced a grin to his lips, then glanced over at her. "We'll talk later. You're beautiful."

She smiled. "And you're handsome. Did I ever tell you that before?"

"No, I don't think you have." Eric put his worries to the back of his mind. For just a little while longer, he wanted to enjoy this day and being with her.

"Guess I was always afraid to. You never told me I was beautiful, either."

"I used to think it a lot, though."

She gripped his hand as it rested on the console between them. "Oh, Eric, I'm so happy!"

"Me, too."

When they reached the club, the courts were nearly empty. They grabbed one of the free ones and began playing. Eric had confessed to her before they had first come to the club together weeks before that he hadn't played much tennis, but Jena never would have guessed. He had strong, angled volleys that always seemed to dip just below Jena's racket, infuriating her, and he had an excellent backhand, too. His whole game was strong, and he kept her running, even though she put her shots where it was hard for him to reach them. She was out of breath after their first set, which Eric won, but she was invigorated, ready to head into a second.

She served, they volleyed, and finally the point was hers. She was determined to beat him this set. They rallied continuously. She ran to catch the shot he had slammed to the opposite side of the court. She ripped it back at him, catching it with the end of her racket. With a hard flick of her wrist, she directed it in a downward path that just cleared the net. He'd never get it, she thought. But he did, popping it over the net. She didn't move fast enough and missed.

"Eric, that's not fair! You were supposed to miss it!"

He laughed, and they resumed playing. Jena won the second set, but just barely.

"Feel like a soda?" Eric asked.

"Love it!"

"I'll be right back."

Jena sat on the bench at the side of the court while Eric went to the clubhouse to get the sodas. As Jena took a towel to wipe the sweat from her forehead, Susan came running over from the other court.

"Jena . . . Jena!" Susan called excitedly.

"Oh, hi, Susan! I didn't see you here."

"You were too busy playing. Oh, but why didn't you tell me!" She came to stand by Jena, her face animated.

"Tell you what?" Jena frowned. "I didn't know we were coming over to play. Eric and I decided on the spur of the moment."

"I mean tell me about Eric! You never told me he was Eric *Clayton—the* Eric Clayton of the Ravens! Oh, Jena, how can you be so blasé about it? You absolutely amaze me! If it was me, I would have been screaming it from the top of the nearest mountain!"

Jena's frown deepened. She shook her head slowly, digesting but hardly daring to believe what Susan was saying.

"You're so lucky," Susan continued. "Most of the girls I know would give their right hand just to *meet* him—and you're *dating* him! And you never even told me . . . didn't even hint."

Eric *Clayton*, Jena was thinking, her mind reeling—not Eric Bliss? How could she have been so blind? No wonder he had looked familiar when she had first seen him—the missing piece of the puzzle. But why had he lied to her? Why? She wanted to scream but didn't want Susan to realize the shock she had just received. Of course, he was Eric Clayton—the connection became clearer and clearer to her as she thought back, remembered the pictures she had seen. No wonder he wouldn't talk about his present life, was so vague. He'd been lying to her— deceiving her! Using her because she was so innocent! Sure, this summer was great fun for him, but in a month or two he would have been gone, leaving Jena in the dust, without her even knowing his real name. She couldn't believe it! Didn't *want* to believe it!

As the pain of the truth sank in, Jena's eyes hardened. She had to pull herself together. She couldn't let Susan see there was anything wrong. She had to find her voice and make some kind of reasonable response.

"I—" she stumbled. "He didn't want me to say anything. You know, the fans and stuff."

"Oh, yeah, really." Susan's eyes were wide. "I can understand. He'd really be mobbed. But you could have told *me,* Jena. I wouldn't have said a word to anyone! Hey, you all right? You look kind of white. I'm sorry if I made you say something you weren't supposed to."

"No, that's OK." Jena's voice was returning to normal. "I know you wouldn't blab it around."

"Never—I won't even tell my brother."

"Don't worry about it, Susan." Jena tried a wavery smile.

Just then Eric reentered the court, his smile easy, a can of soda in each hand.

The girls started; Susan's eyes widened further, if that was possible.

Eric looked at Susan, grinned, handed Jena her soda. "Hi. A friend of yours, Jena?"

"Yes. Eric, I'd like you to meet Susan Strasberg. You've heard me talk about her."

Eric nodded, extending his hand. "Nice to meet you, Susan."

"And Susan," Jena continued, forcing her voice to be as normal as possible, "this is Eric Clayton." She put only the slightest emphasis on the last name.

Eric already had Susan's hand when Jena's use of his real name registered. The smile was wiped from his lips. He swung his head toward Jena, who was staring at him coldly, her features set.

Susan, so excited to be meeting Eric Clayton in the flesh, didn't even notice the look that passed between the two. She was bubbling. "It's so fantastic to meet you! Could I—would it be too pushy to ask for your autograph?"

Eric was tempted to say there had been some mistake. The words were on the tip of his tongue, but he knew from the look in Jena's eyes that it was too late. Adding another lie to his pile would only make matters worse.

He nodded absentmindedly to Susan. "Yeah . . . sure . . ."

"I'll be right back," Susan said gaily. "I just have to get my bag."

As she rushed off, Eric turned to Jena. "Jena, please, I'm sorry. I was going to tell you. . . ."

"I don't think we have anything to say to each other."

"Jena, listen—at least let me tell you my side of the story."

"More lies? I don't want to hear them." She was having trouble fighting back the tears.

"No lies. Please, Jena—the truth this time. . . ."

Susan burst back into the court, still oblivious to the undercurrents. "Here, I've found a pen and paper. Oh, I really appreciate this. I just wish I had one of your albums with me!"

Eric forced his attention to the bubbling girl. "Susan, wasn't it?" If he had been in another state of mind, he might have written something more creative, but he was finding it impossible to concentrate on anything but Jena, her anger, his own shock and fear.

"Oh, thanks. Thanks so much!" Susan said as he handed the paper back to her. "And I won't say anything to anyone that you're here. I promise!"

He forced a smile.

Jena got to her feet quickly. "Eric, I think I'd

better get home." She picked up her racket and tennis bag. "Susan, I'll be talking to you."

"Yeah. Bye, Jena. Bye, Eric—and thanks. Great to meet you!"

Jena was already striding toward the car, and Eric hurried after her. What was he going to say? How could he explain when she didn't even want to listen to him? What a mess he'd gotten himself into. What a fool he'd been.

Chapter Fourteen

Without a word, Jena climbed into the passenger seat of the Ferrari, slamming the door after her. Here was another lie, she thought. Sure, he was taking care of the car for someone. Like someone would really trust a college kid with their Ferrari. How gullible she had been!

Eric got in, his expression tense, his mouth tight. He took one look at Jena's stony profile, then started the car.

Eric felt a lump in his throat. He headed the car away from the club, roaring down the highway in his frustration. He didn't know how to begin. Finally the words burst out of his mouth.

"Jena, please, I know you're angry. You have every right to be. But I *was* going to tell you. I tried to this morning, but then you said you wanted to play tennis."

"Sure," Jena said coldly.

"Look, I'm not going to make excuses. I should have told you long before today. I know that. Jena, I came down here this summer to get away from it all. I never expected to meet anyone. I took the name Eric Bliss so no one would guess I was here. I was exhausted; I needed a break. It never occurred to me that day I met you on the beach that anything would come of it. And then—then—"

"And then you just kept on lying and lying! Why didn't you tell me the next day when you came up to La Paloma? You had all the opportunity in the world! And I would have understood, Eric—easily!" All Jena could think was that he had been using her. He had never intended to tell her. He was a famous rock star. He had more exciting girls in his life than Jena Maxwell.

"It's so hard to explain, Jena. I have a whole different life out there."

"No kidding!"

"Listen! Since I got in with the Ravens, my private life really isn't my own—in fact, I don't have a private life. When you and I started getting friendly, I just couldn't see how it could go anywhere. I tried to keep it friendly so that when I left, it wouldn't matter whether you knew me by my real name or not."

122

"It still would have mattered! Do you think I would have forgotten all about you just because we were only friends? How unfair!"

"I was wrong. I know it. You deserved the truth, whether we were just friends, or more. But when I started to realize how much I cared for you, then I was afraid to tell you—afraid you'd walk off and end it. I kept putting it off . . . until yesterday when I knew I couldn't put it off any longer."

"You didn't mean that, either, did you?" Jena felt like crying. "You get your kicks playing with dumb, naive kids like me? Ha, ha, here I am a big star," she said sneeringly, "and here's this little jerk, falling in love with me. Oh, well, another one to add to your list!"

"It's not like that!" Eric yelled, trying to get through to her. "I don't think that way at all. I've fooled around, sure, but that was in the past. Jena, I meant what I said. I love you."

"Try your lies on some other little girl, Eric. I've had all I can take."

"But I'm telling you the truth."

"Funny, but I find it so hard to believe you."

"If you'd give me a chance. . . ."

They had reached La Paloma. Eric pulled to a stop, then turned in his seat toward Jena to emphasize the importance of his words. She refused to look at him. He reached out for her, but she already had her fingers on the door handle.

"You can say all you want now, Eric, but I know you never intended to see me again after this summer." She jumped out of the car and rushed for the front of the house.

"Jena, please, stay! No. Jena. We can straighten this out!"

She paused at the front door and looked back at him. "Go back to your world, Eric, and all your pretty ladies who know how to play your game!"

The front door slammed behind her with finality.

Eric dropped his head on the steering wheel. He hadn't cried since he was ten years old, but he felt like crying now. And he had no one to blame but himself. If only she would listen to him—believe him. Oh, what did it matter? Why was he getting upset about one lousy girl? he asked himself. But that didn't help, either. In frustration and anger at himself, he threw the Ferrari into gear and tore out of the driveway in a cloud of dust.

Jena ran upstairs to her room and threw herself on her bed. She could hear Eric's car racing away, and although she had told him to leave, the sound intensified her pain. She was too involved in the situation to see anything logically. All she could think about was how he had lied to her, not just a small white lie, but a constant *big* lie. She had told him she loved him; she had opened her heart to him, and he

124

had humiliated her, embarrassed her. She felt as though he'd seen her innocence and used it to his advantage. She found it impossible to believe, with all his other lies, that he could have been telling the truth when he'd said he loved her. It hurt so much. She wasn't going to let him make a fool of her again! But despite her determination, the sobs came, and she buried her face in her pillow.

Eric called that night, but even Maria's most earnest pleas couldn't persuade Jena to come to the phone. Jena didn't explain the details to Maria, only that she and Eric had had a fight and she wasn't speaking to him. It took all Jena's willpower not to give in when she knew Eric was on the phone. Maybe it wouldn't hurt just to listen to what he had to say. But, no, what could he tell her she didn't already know?

She left the house early the next morning to play tennis with Susan, and dreading a return to La Paloma, where she'd be alone with her thoughts, she accepted Susan's invitation to come over to her house, meet her family, and listen to some records. When she returned home later that afternoon, she learned that Eric had been over to see her and finding her out, had sat down at the kitchen table with Maria and talked. He explained everything—his deception, the guilt he was feeling, his overwhelming desire to patch things up. As he left he asked Maria to *please* have Jena call him when she got home.

Maria met Jena at the door and told her of Eric's visit. She saw Jena's face grow tense, but Maria wouldn't let Jena run up to her room until the girl had heard her out.

"He's such a nice boy, Jena," Maria said earnestly, "and he is truly sorry. We all make mistakes. Won't you at least listen to him? Talk to him?"

"I could never believe him again, Maria, or trust him."

"This is your first time with love. I know what it is like; I remember my own first love. We tend to expect too much from it, from the other person—"

"It's no good," Jena interrupted, her voice brusque to hide the tears that were threatening her. "He hurt me."

"At least think about it. Give him a chance."

Shaking her head, Jena hurried away. The tears were too close to the surface. She was right—she was sure she was right in her judgment, and she was afraid that if she ever trusted him again, he could hurt her even more.

When Eric called again that evening, Maria, following Jena's instructions, told him Jena wasn't at home. Maria had no choice. Jena had adamantly refused to come to the phone.

"Then take a message, will you, Maria?" Eric's tone reflected his misery and disappointment.

"Sí, of course I will."

"I've just had a call from Los Angeles. Something unexpected has come up, and I have to leave Del Costa tomorrow morning. I can't leave a number where she can reach me because I may be traveling around, but I'll call her as soon as I can, and, Maria, ask her to please reconsider."

"I will, Eric. I will try my best."

"Thanks, Maria. I'll call soon."

"Sí. Goodbye, Eric."

"Bye."

Chapter Fifteen

The days passed slowly for Jena. The hurt that had wrapped itself around her like a blanket was increasing, not lessening, and she had been having second thoughts. Maybe she should have given Eric the benefit of the doubt. Perhaps she had been too stubborn. She missed him so much. It was almost impossible to believe that in a few short weeks he had come to mean so much to her and had made such an impact on her life. Her days seemed empty. As much as she tried to keep herself too busy to think, it wasn't the same without him, and she couldn't control the thoughts that invaded her mind.

Perhaps she should have believed him. Perhaps he *had* been planning to tell her the truth, and she had been mistaken. Jena didn't know what to think. She only waited anxiously for his call. This time she would talk to him, and maybe together they could sort it all out.

In the meantime, she read every rock magazine she could lay her hands on, listened to all the Ravens' albums, concentrating on the guitar, trying to pick out his voice. While Jena had always liked music, she had never paid more than passing interest to the recording stars, especially individual members of rock groups. She knew certain faces and names, which was why Eric had seem familiar, but she had never shared Susan's fascination with the intricacies of their personal lives and backgrounds. Now, with the help of Susan's magazine collection, Jena was learning a great deal about the real Eric Clayton. The articles told of his background in Wyoming, which she already knew, and talked of his coming to Los Angeles and his first contact with the Ravens. This she read with interest. It was a part of Eric's life that was a mystery to her. Some of the more gossipy articles mentioned girlfriends—different starlets with whom he had been linked, but even to Jena's tormented eyes, these seemed more supposition than fact. Reading about him, seeing his face in photos brought conflicting emotions, but it was a kind of tortured joy she couldn't resist.

Since Eric's departure, Jena's friendship with Susan had steadily grown. Not only was it important to Jena to have a girl her age with whom to talk, but Susan was really nice, and she shared a lot of common interests with Jena. When Jena had broken down and told Susan the real story about herself and Eric, Susan had been totally sympathetic. She could see why Jena thought she had been used, but she could see Eric's side, too.

"I think he really cares," Susan told her one afternoon as they were sitting on Susan's back patio sunning themselves.

"Why do you say that?"

"He wouldn't have tried so hard to get in touch with you and explain if he didn't care."

Jena could see her point. She had been thinking about that, too. "Maybe he just felt guilty."

"He wouldn't go to those lengths—and look at the message he left with Maria for you, asking you to please reconsider."

"Yeah . . . I know. But he's been gone a week now. You'd think he would have called. He's probably back with his famous friends and has forgotten all about me—or at least has decided it isn't worth all the trouble I've been giving him."

"I don't think so." Susan sounded so positive. If only Jena could feel the same confidence.

"And he told me," Jena continued stubbornly, "that he didn't have any private life. He's dedicated to his career, and that doesn't leave any room for girlfriends. He's probably just as happy that he got out of it."

"Wait and see." Susan remained optimistic. "He'll call. And this time you'd better talk to him!"

"I will," Jena said emphatically. "I will."

But when Eric's call came through, Jena wasn't at home.

"I'm so sorry, Eric." Maria was sincerely upset. "You just missed her. She left in the car only a few minutes ago. I'll have her call you?"

"No. I'm at a phone booth in the airport. My flight leaves in a few minutes. We're on our way to a concert in Houston. Listen, tell her I'll call her from there as soon as I can, later this afternoon."

"I will, Eric. Take care of yourself."

"You too, Maria."

As soon as he'd hung up, Maria immediately dialed the Strasbergs', where Jena had been headed when she left the ranch that morning.

"Mrs. Strasberg?" Maria spoke into the phone.

"Yes."

"This is Maria Juarez, the housekeeper at La Paloma. Is Jena there?"

"Well, she was, but I sent Susan and her on some errands for me in La Jolla. They'll probably be a few hours. I hope you don't mind."

"No, no." Maria frowned. "It's only that she received an important phone call. Will you tell her as soon as she returns that Eric called and

131

she should come right home, since he will be calling back later today?"

"Of course, Maria, I'd be glad to. I'll send her right home."

"Yes, it's very important, and thank you, Mrs. Strasberg."

"You're quite welcome."

But Marge Strasberg could be scatterbrained at times, and when Susan and Jena returned, she had completely forgotten the message. She was busy working in her garden and barely even noticed the girls as they brought in her packages and then went up to Susan's room to talk.

Eric called back at four. Maria was beside herself when she picked up the phone and heard his voice.

"Can I speak to Jena, Maria?"

"She's not home yet."

"Did you tell her I called?"

"I left a message, but—"

"But my call wasn't important enough for her to come home."

"No, Eric—"

"Forget it, Maria. It's not your fault. I guess I've got the picture." His tone was icy.

"No, Eric, wait!"

But the line was dead. Maria heard the buzz of the dial tone, stood staring at the receiver for a long moment before she returned it to its cradle. What was she going to tell Jena? Why hadn't the girl come home? After telling Maria that she wanted to talk to Eric, had Jena changed her mind yet again? Maria shook her head sadly. What problems the young could make for themselves.

It was five o'clock before Jena left the Strasbergs. She had just driven out of sight when Marge Strasberg suddenly slapped her palm against her forehead and exclaimed to her daughter, "Oh, my goodness. I forgot all about the phone call."

"Phone call?"

"Maria, the housekeeper at La Paloma, called when you were in La Jolla this morning. She said Jena was to come home as soon as you got back. Some boy." She shook her head. "I can't remember his name. Anyway, he was calling this afternoon. It completely slipped my mind."

"Oh, mother." Susan moaned, closing her eyes. "How could you forget?"

"I *am* sorry. But I know these boys. I'm sure he'll call back."

"No . . ." Susan sighed. "This was different. Didn't Maria say it was important?"

"Well, she may have said something like that."

Susan looked at her mother in exasperation. "Why didn't you write it down? You know Daddy got you that message board just for that reason."

"Oh, yes, but I was on my way out to the garden. . . ."

133

"Poor Jena." Susan shook her head. "I hope she's in time."

Jena drove home in happy spirits. She had this feeling, which she didn't fully understand, that things were going to work out all right between Eric and her. And she knew exactly what she wanted to say to him when he did call.

She entered the kitchen humming, looking for a snack to hold her over until dinner. "Hi, Maria. What's for supper?"

Jena was unprepared for the mournful, sad-eyed look Maria gave her.

"What's wrong, Maria?"

"Oh, Jena, why didn't you come home?"

"But I'm here."

"Before—in time for his call."

"What call?"

"My message. I told Mrs. Strasberg."

"She didn't say anything about you calling."

"But how could she not? I said it was important!"

"She's very forgetful. Nice lady, but—what's all this about? What was so important?"

"Eric—"

"*He called!*" Jena's voice was jubilant. "He's calling back? You got a number?"

"No—yes—I mean he did call back. Let me tell you it all." Maria sat down wearily at the kitchen table. "He called right after you left for Susan's.

I said you were out and asked for his number. He was at the airport and said he would call you later this afternoon when he got to Houston. I telephoned Mrs. Strasberg. She said you had gone to La Jolla. I told her it was important that you come right home when you returned, that Eric had called and was calling back. She said fine, she would tell you. I waited and waited, not knowing if you had changed your mind and no longer wanted to talk to him. Then he called again at four. When I said you were still out, he gave me no chance to explain, to get his number. He just said he guessed he got the picture and hung up. Oh, Jena, I am so sorry. I tried to stop him, to tell him. . . ."

Jena had by now slumped down in the chair next to Maria's, her face in her hands.

"Did he say he'd call again?" She knew he hadn't, but she didn't want to give up that last thread of hope.

Maria shook her head, her eyes sad.

"He sounded angry?"

Maria nodded.

"And hung up on you?"

"Yes."

"Thinking I was up to my old games. Oh, no." Jena felt her throat closing. She wanted to cry. "He said he was going to Houston?"

"Sí, I believe that was the city."

"Did he say what for?"

"Ah, yes." Maria brightened momentarily. "He was going to a concert."

"They're on tour then," Jena said more to herself. "But he didn't say where they were playing—where he was staying?"

"No—nothing."

Jena knew then it was hopeless. Eric wouldn't be calling back, and she had no way of getting in touch with him. They could be performing anywhere in Houston. It was a huge city. The tears started sliding down her cheeks. "I think I'll go to my room."

"I am so sorry, Jena. I tried."

"I know you did. It's not your fault. It's nobody's fault but my own. If I'd talked to him in the beginning—" She choked back a sob. "Well, it's too late now." Jena pushed herself up from the table. "I don't think I want anything for dinner, Maria. I've suddenly lost my appetite."

Wisely, Maria didn't protest. Let the girl cry it out. Perhaps she would feel better. Oh, but how unfortunate life could sometimes be.

Chapter Sixteen

Susan called Jena the next morning. She had waited impatiently for news from her friend, hoping for the best, but when she hadn't heard by ten, she realized something was wrong.

She listened unhappily as Jena told her what had happened.

"Do you want to come over, Jena?"

"Why don't you come here? I want to go down to the beach where I met him. It's probably self-torture. . . ." There was a moment's silence. "Think you'll be OK to ride that far?"

"Sure," Susan responded. "My riding teacher gave me four stars this week. Good practice, anyway. I'll leave in a few minutes."

"Thanks, Susan."

"Anytime. I know you'd do the same thing for me."

Jena was waiting by the stables when Susan pulled in. Diablo and a quiet mare were saddled and waiting. She felt numb. Her eyes, still sore and red from a night spent sobbing into her pillow, were narrowed against the bright sunlight. Her full, pretty mouth drooped at the corners; her usual liveliness was veiled in a cloud of listlessness. When she turned to greet Susan, her smile was weak and distracted.

Susan was concerned. "You sure you're all right?"

"As right as I can be under the circumstances. I had Max saddle up Amy for you. She's nice and quiet and won't give you any trouble."

"You really want to go down to the beach?"

"Yes." Jena's answer was so firm, Susan didn't dare question her further.

Jena was silent until they were mounted up and heading away from the ranch buildings. "I'm not very good company."

"That's OK. I wish there was something I could say to make you feel better. My mother said to apologize to you. She's really sorry. She didn't forget intentionally. . . . Well, you know what she's like."

"She had no way of knowing how important the call was. Everyone forgets things sometimes."

"But of all messages. . . ." Susan let the sentence drift. No point in reminding Jena of that.

"At least my summer didn't turn out as boring as I thought it would be." Jena smiled bitterly, though she wasn't looking for sympathy.

"It could have been worse."

"I've been reminding myself of that. Have you ever been hurt by a guy, Susan?"

"Once—last year. But it wasn't really a big thing. At first I thought it was the end of the world. I moped around for a few weeks, but I don't think I really loved him. My pride was hurt more than anything else."

"That's different then."

"From the way you feel?"

"Yeah." Jena reined Diablo around a boulder. "But you got over it?"

"Sure. In a couple of weeks another guy asked me out, and I forgot all about Barry. Well, not entirely, but it didn't hurt anymore to see him with another girl."

Jena sighed. "But where I'm going, back to girls' school, I'm not likely to meet any guys."

"Aren't there any boys' schools around? I've heard where they have these joint dances."

"Not Chase. Too straight for that. We are there, according to our headmistress, 'to get an education, not to become acquainted with the opposite

139

sex,' " Jena said, mimicking the headmistress's nasal voice.

"Still, a lot of things could happen. You weren't expecting to meet Eric this summer." Susan could have bit her tongue after the words were out of her mouth.

"I suppose."

When they reached the beach, Jena pulled Diablo up on the crest overlooking it. Susan pulled up alongside.

"Pretty, isn't it?" Jena asked.

"Sure is."

"Right over there"—Jena pointed to a spot on the sand—"is where I first saw Eric."

Susan was silent for a moment. "He still might call again." But even she didn't sound convinced.

"After the way I've acted? If our situations were reversed, I wouldn't call him."

"But he's got to realize you had a good right to be angry and needed time to think it through."

"I told him I never wanted to see him again and that nothing he could say would change my mind." Jena sighed. "If only there was some way I could get in touch with him."

"You could write his record company. They must have an address in L.A."

"They'd think it was another fan letter. He'd never see it."

"If you marked it personal?"

"Susan, do you realize how many letters the

Ravens must get each week? And his fans have probably tried every gimmick in the book to get their letters to him personally."

Susan was thoughtful for a moment. "I have an idea," she said at last. "I'll talk to my father— of course, I won't tell him about you—but he has a lot of contacts in the entertainment business. Maybe he could get you an address."

"Do you think?" For a moment there was a spark of hope in Jena's eyes. "If I could explain to him, tell him I understand why he had to lie, tell him how I feel. . . ." Her voice drifted off. "At least I'll have tried, and if I don't hear from him, I'll know exactly where I stand. I guess the hardest thing is not knowing what he's thinking, whether he still cares or if I've turned him off completely."

Susan was silent. It was her personal feeling that Eric did care and that his feelings couldn't have changed that quickly or easily. Yet it was only a feeling. She had come into the situation too late to really know, and she didn't want to raise Jena's hopes without reason.

The weeks passed slowly. Jena tried to keep her mind off Eric, but it was impossible. She couldn't help but hope that maybe, just maybe, Eric might try to call her again. Every time the phone rang, her heart started racing, but one day followed another, and no call came, no letter, and she finally faced up to the fact that she wasn't going to hear from him. The summer was almost over. In the fall she would be on the East Coast, completely out of his reach.

Susan had talked to her father, but his connections were more in the movie industry. He didn't know anyone who could give him an inside address where a letter would end up in Eric's hands. He said he'd be happy to get them tickets, though, if the Ravens were ever playing in the area.

Jena occupied herself with as many things as she could to keep her mind off Eric, but everywhere she went there was always some little reminder. She had traveled most of the trails on the ranch with him on their outings. She would see a landmark and remember some comment he'd made. At the tennis courts she couldn't help but be reminded of their last afternoon together. Even the comfortable kitchen at La Paloma brought memories of the night of her accident and the many other times Eric had sat around it with Max, Pepe, and Maria. She gave Susan back all of her rock magazines and put away her own collection of Ravens albums. If one of their songs came on the car radio, she immediately flicked it off.

Time hung heavily on her hands. Sometimes she wished the summer was over and she was in a plane that had no reminders of Eric, but then again, she didn't want the separation between them to be that final.

Then a week before Jena's scheduled departure for New York, Susan called her excitedly on the phone.

"Jena, I've got the best news! You won't believe it!"

"You've talked your parents into sending you back to L.A. for school."

"You know that since I met Willie, I don't want to go back to L.A. for school. No, this is something really exciting. You'll never guess!"

"I probably won't."

"The Ravens are in concert in L.A. this weekend!"

Silence on the other end of the phone. Just the mention of the name was enough to start Jena's heart thumping.

"Jena, did you hear me?"

"Yes, I heard you."

"You don't sound very excited."

"Susan—"

"No, wait, listen. I haven't told you the best part. Daddy's gotten us tickets—front row—the best seats in the house. See, he remembered when I asked a couple of weeks ago—"

"He's gotten us tickets?" Jena's voice was stunned, disbelieving.

"Yes, for Sunday. You don't have to go back to New York until next Thursday, right?"

"Right."

"Listen, Jena. This will be your chance. Eric will be there."

"*I* know that." She couldn't think clearly. To see Eric again. Her mouth went dry. She was suddenly afraid. It was what she had wanted, but he would be on stage. Would she even have a chance to see him in person?

"You can talk to him," Susan continued blissfully, "explain everything."

"And how do you plan to arrange the meeting? Or should I just jump right up on stage and say, 'Eric, here I am'?"

"We'll go to the stage door afterward."

"With the rest of the mob? You *have* heard of groupies, haven't you, Susan?"

"Don't be so negative. We'll find a way, even if I have to hold a sign over your head announcing you."

"You wouldn't dare!"

"Of course I wouldn't, but, Jena, what do you say? Will you go?"

Jena was tempted, but she was afraid that seeing him again, being so close yet so far away, would only make her hurt that much more.

"I'm not taking no for an answer. I'll come and drag you to the concert!"

Jena hesitated. Her brain was spinning. Finally she knew what she had to do. "OK, I'll go."

"You won't be sorry!" Susan gave a whoop. "Daddy's letting me take the car. The concert starts at two, so we should leave here about eleven so I can find a place to park and everything."

"OK—OK," Jena answered mechanically. Her mind was filled with the thought of seeing Eric again. Would she have a chance to talk to him?

Chapter Seventeen

The girls left for Los Angeles promptly at eleven. Susan was excited; Jena was so nervous she kept clenching and unclenching her hands in her lap to try to release some of her tension. What if, after all of this, she didn't get anywhere near Eric? What if she saw him and he told her to get lost? Of course, there were the happier possibilities to consider, too, but she was afraid to get her hopes up.

"There'll be three groups playing in the concert," Susan remarked as she swung up onto the freeway. "The Ravens are the second group up, and with our seats we should be able to see everything."

"I'm scared, Susan."

"That's normal. I'd be scared, too, if I were

146

you, but everything's going to work out great, believe me, Jena."

"I'm trying to think of the good side. Do I look all right?" Jena glanced down nervously at the wraparound skirt and full-sleeved blouse she had worn.

"You look fantastic. I told you that before. Like a model."

"But do you think I'm too dressed up? I probably should have worn jeans. I had them on and changed my mind."

"Everyone will be in jeans. You'll stand out."

"That's what I'm afraid of."

"Who are you trying to impress? Eric or the audience?"

"Eric."

"OK."

Traffic wasn't bad, and the drive took only a little over two hours.

"Do you know your way?" Jena asked.

"Sure do." Susan laughed. "Don't forget, this is my old stomping ground. I should be able to find a place to park right up here. We may have to walk a little way, but we have time."

Jena checked her watch. "One-fifteen."

They found a space to park in the lot adjoining the concert hall. They locked the car, then began walking toward the hall. They could see a large crowd already gathered at the door.

Unable to still the butterflies that were flapping around in her stomach, Jena took a deep

147

breath. "I'm so nervous, Susan, I feel like I'm going to get sick."

For a second Susan looked alarmed. "Want to go to the ladies' room?"

"No, I guess I'll be all right once we sit down."

Susan produced the tickets, and in a moment an usher was leading them down to their front-row center seats. Already it was obvious there wasn't going to be an empty seat in the house. There was a loud, excited hum of noise and laughter all around as the crowd poured in.

"I'm glad we got here early," Susan commented.

"Me, too." But Jena couldn't relax. It wasn't until the first group came on stage, a little-known lead-in band for the Ravens, that she felt some of the tension easing out of her muscles. The group was good and finished to cheers and loud applause, but just like Jena, the audience was keyed up and waiting with expectation for the Ravens and the group following them, the Asteroids.

Jena waited impatiently through the intermission, then the house lights dimmed, and the Ravens walked out on stage. Jena instantly spotted Eric. But he looked so different! He was wearing tight white pants and a glittering, long-sleeved shirt that was open to his waist. He had his guitar slung over his shoulder as he bent down to adjust the knobs on one of the amplifiers. Jena's heart was beating so fast, she thought it was going to jump right out of her chest.

Already the audience was going wild—screaming, yelling, whistling.

The other Ravens took their positions. The drummer and keyboard player were to the back, and in the front by three standing microphones were Eric, then the lead vocalist, who Jena knew filled in on flute, and lastly the bass guitarist. The loudspeaker system buzzed as the instruments were tuned and the sound adjusted. The stage lights went on in a kaleidoscope of colors with spots directed at each of the band members. Then the lead vocalist came forward.

"The Ravens want. . . ." The rest of his words were drowned out by the load roar that went up in the crowd, the cheers, the clapping. Finally, shaking his head and laughing, he motioned to the other Ravens, and they went immediately into their first number, a fast rock piece with a driving rhythm that vibrated through the huge hall. The song was one of Jena's favorites, and she gripped the arms of her chair.

The lead singer was featured. As he belted out the fast-paced lyrics, Jena saw Eric's eyes watching him, dropping from time to time to his guitar strings. He wasn't looking out into the audience at all, but Jena watched every movement of his fingers, every sway of his body to the rhythm of the music. Then Eric was leaning over the mike, joining in the singing.

149

Jena was suddenly conscious of his voice—it was ringing in her ears. It blended with the lead singer's, yet Eric's voice was all she heard. As the Ravens swung into their next number, Jena clapped so hard her palms hurt.

Eric was facing out toward the audience now. She saw him looking out over her head to the mass of faces, a crooked grin on his lips—that sleepy smile she so loved. He'd never see her, she thought feverishly. With the glare of the lights, and all the people. . . .

The band was doing one of their ballads. She heard Eric's voice again, singing the lyrics. "Why . . . why . . . why can't we love again. Bring the sun back into my heart. . . ."

She froze. It was as though the words were meant for her. They were the words she would have sung to him. But he didn't even know she was there. It was just a song.

She was concentrating on him so hard, she was sure he must have felt the vibrations. Then Eric dropped his eyes, away from the back-row seats, to those directly in front of the stage. His gaze swept along, face to face. Audience contact— that was what it was called. Jena was sure he wasn't actually seeing individuals, but in the next instant he was looking directly at her. Her heart was beating so quickly, she couldn't even smile, only stare. She realized that the easy grin had suddenly been wiped from his lips, that his eyes had widened. His hand faltered on

150

his guitar strings. Quickly he swung his head away, concentrated on the music, regained his composure.

Yet in a moment his eyes were back on her face. There was a question in them. They were narrowed, as if he were trying to see more clearly through the blinding spotlights.

Susan poked Jena in the ribs; she was whispering excitedly. "He sees you, Jena! He knows it's you!"

"Yes . . . yes." Jena's throat felt constricted; her lips felt frozen; she couldn't seem to move.

"Didn't I tell you!"

Eric was still staring. The question in his eyes called for a response. Despite the demands of the performance, he was concentrating his attention on her.

Was he really seeing her? Was that really recognition in his eyes? Did she dare signal to him, raise her hand? Then suddenly she couldn't stop herself. Her lips spread in a joyous smile. Unconsciously, her hand shot up into the air; she blew him a kiss.

There was a moment's startled pause, then Eric's white teeth flashed in the spotlight, his grin brilliant, ear to ear. He threw back his head as though in relief and happiness. Jena had the feeling that if it hadn't been for his surroundings, he would have shouted. But Eric was too much a professional.

Yet for the rest of the performance, his eyes

never strayed far from Jena. His playing and singing and movements had a new life and feeling, and the broad smile never left his lips.

The charm and magnetism he was sending out reached others in the audience. Jena could heard the girls' cries all around her. "Eric! More, Eric!" She felt a stab of jealousy, then pride. That was the Eric she knew and cared for up there. The Eric she hoped still cared for her, too. He was magnificent!

Jena couldn't believe how quickly the end came, how soon the Ravens were playing an encore, then were taking their final bows to a standing ovation, calls, cheers.

Some fans had brought flowers, and handfuls of them were now raining down on the stage. Eric picked up one blossom that had dropped to the stage at his feet, raised it to his lips, and tossed it right into Jena's lap. Then the Ravens made their exit.

The house lights went on, signaling the intermission, but Jena sat frozen in a state of shock. She held the flower in her fingers, touched it to her own lips. Susan, too, seemed stunned. Then she was hugging Jena, almost crying in her excitement for her friend.

"Yippee! I'm so happy for you!"

"Do you think he still loves me, Susan? I mean he threw the flower. . . ."

"I'd say there's a pretty good chance. Did you see the way he was watching you? Wow, I'd die!

And I'd say there are a few other girls around here who wish they were you. Did you hear them screaming when the flower landed in your lap?"

"Yeah." Jena managed to laugh. "I heard them. I was almost afraid they'd come and grab it out of my hand."

"No, this is a pretty sane crowd. Better than I've seen at most concerts."

"What do I do now?" Suddenly the fact had sunk in that Eric was no longer on the stage, that he was closed up in some dressing room. He was the celebrity, while she was just another member of the audience.

"We can go to the stage door," Susan responded quickly. "He's bound to look for you. We could even leave now. I don't mind missing the Asteroids."

"I don't know." Jena hesitated. She was sure Eric would make some effort to contact her. She just didn't know whether she should make the first move or wait for him.

The decision was taken out of her hands. A guy in jeans and a plaid shirt was bending over in front of her.

"You Jena Maxwell?"

"Yes."

"Got this message for you. From Eric Clayton."

"Oh! Thank you."

"He said to wait."

153

"OK. Let me read it." Jena's fingers trembled as she unfolded the sheet of paper and read the note.

Jena,

I didn't believe my eyes. But there couldn't be two girls in the world who look like you. I hope I'm right in thinking your coming means you're ready to talk to me. Will you meet me backstage? Teddy will bring you.

As ever,
Eric

Jena looked up, her insides jumping around in excitement. "Teddy?"

"Yeah."

"Can you wait half a second?" Jena turned to Susan, who was all eyes and ears. "Eric wants me to meet him—now. Do you want to stay here?"

"Of course, I'll stay here. I don't want to interrupt. Where are you meeting him?"

"Backstage."

"Then listen. If you're not finished in time to meet me back here, which I doubt you will be, meet me at the car or leave a note or something."

"OK." Jena couldn't think straight. She squeezed Susan's hand quickly in thanks. "See you later." Then she grabbed her shoulder bag and followed Teddy.

He led her out the side door to the left of the

stage, back through a door marked Private Personnel Only, and down a narrow hallway. At its end the hallway widened into a rectangular area with some chairs to either side and doorways breaking the wall every six feet or so. Each door had a number and was marked Dressing Room. There were about a dozen people milling about, talking, laughing, drinking coffee.

"Wait here." Teddy motioned her to a chair, then went to a door at the far end. He rapped with his knuckles on the wood. The door opened a crack. Jena heard Teddy's low mumble but could pick out no distinct words or the response coming from the other side of the door. Teddy nodded, turned, and walked back to Jena.

"He'll be with you in a minute." He smiled quickly. "Guess you're not one of the usual." He flushed.

"Definitely not."

"Well, good luck. Have a good time—whatever." He flung up his hands. "He's a pretty good guy. More down to earth than the usual egomaniacs we get in here."

"I know. And thanks, Teddy."

He grinned again, nodded, then moved quickly off and retreated through one of the doors in the hall.

Jena sat there feeling out of place. Everyone seemed to know each other. The wait seemed endless. She was nervous about seeing Eric again, and her hands were trembling. Eric on stage had seemed delighted to see her, but what would he have to say when they met? Would he accept her apology for judging him too quickly? Seeing him up on stage, radiating magnetism, performing with such energy and talent had made Jena distinctly aware of who he was—that the Eric she had met on the beach was the person underneath, but this was his other side. This was the Eric she had never imagined existed during their relationship. She felt as though the ground had been pulled out from under her. Not until this afternoon, when she had seen him charming the audience and building them to a pitch of excitement, had Eric Clayton the rock star seemed completely real.

She slid a mirror from her bag and quickly studied her face. Her hair was still smoothly brushed and glowing as it fell on her shoulders in heavy, soft waves. In all the excitement she hadn't bitten off her lipstick, and her cheeks were flushed with anticipation. She dropped her mirror back in her bag.

The door creaked open at the end of the hall.

Jena looked up. Her face showed every bit of her nervousness . . . her happiness, too. She watched the door. Then a figure, dressed in jeans and an open-necked shirt, stepped through.

He looked over the people gathered about. Several people complimented him on his performance, and although he smiled and thanked them, his eyes were searching for Jena.

Jena was so overwhelmed, seeing him at last in the flesh after dreaming of him so long, she didn't know whether to sit, stand, or walk forward. But he spotted her and walked toward her, his steps picking up speed, his face brightening from the serious look it had worn as he had stepped through the door.

"Jena! Goldilocks!" He held out his arms.

And she ran into them. "Oh, Eric!"

"It's been too long." His arms closed about her as they met.

"I know. There's so much I have to tell you."

He rubbed his cheeks against her ear. "I missed you, Jena."

"I missed you, too. You were wonderful out there."

"Did you think so?"

"Yes." She was so choked up she could barely talk.

"We have to talk. Let's go for a ride somewhere. Can you?"

"Yes! Yes. I just have to leave a note for Susan. I came up with her. She got the tickets. She's been a good friend to me."

"I'll have to thank her for that. My car is out back, heavily guarded." He grinned. "We'll have to sneak out, although there shouldn't be too much of a mob scene because most people will be staying to hear the Asteroids."

"Let me just write a note for Susan and leave it on her windshield. When will we be back?"

"I'll drive you home."

"To La Paloma?"

"To La Paloma. I've been thinking about it a lot these last weeks. Write your note."

Jena scribbled quickly on a piece of paper she had found in her bag. She hoped Susan would be OK on the long drive home by herself, but she couldn't give up this chance to be with Eric.

After she had written her note, Eric led her out a side entrance. He waited at the doorway while Jena hurried through the parking lot to Susan's car. She fastened her message securely under the windshield wiper, then returned to where Eric was waiting.

"My car's over there, behind the fence. No one's going to expect me to come out this door, but I don't want to take a chance on getting stopped. We're going to have to run."

"Let's go!" Jena said excitedly.

He laughed and grabbed her hand as they went sprinting toward the fence.

Chapter Eighteen

Jena's high-heeled sandals weren't meant for that kind of exercise, but she kept up with Eric as they made their way to the fenced compound. There were more people outside than Eric had expected. Several people looked at them and recognized Eric but no one had a chance to come near him—he and Jena were moving too fast. They reached the gates, and Eric quickly showed the guard a card. They were admitted to the private area.

His Ferrari stood under a palm tree, but Jena wasn't conscious of anything except that she was with him.

He drove toward Santa Monica. They said little to each other during the drive, knowing that soon enough they would be talking freely. Eric's hand clasped hers tightly. Once he lifted it and touched it to his lips, then he concentrated on his driving.

He pulled up on a high cliff overlooking the Santa Monica beach. It wasn't the quietest of places, but the view was magnificent. There were people around, a lot of tourists, but they weren't paying attention to Eric and Jena, and Eric and Jena weren't paying attention to them. The crowds didn't exist.

Eric turned off the ignition, rested his hands on the steering wheel for a moment, then swiveled toward her.

"Now tell me, Jena," he said quietly, "why you came today."

Her voice was equally soft, almost hesitant as she looked into his face. "The last time you phoned, Eric, I was waiting for your call. I wanted to tell you I was sorry, that I'd been too abrupt. I wanted to tell you I understood why you'd lied and why it went on for so long—and to tell you I still loved you. But I was out at Susan's, and Susan's mother forgot to tell me about the message Maria had left. I never knew you'd called until I got home that night—and then it was too late."

She cleared her throat and brushed a strand of hair from her face. "Maria told me how angry you were, and that you'd gone to Houston on tour. But I didn't know how to get in touch with you, or where. I wanted to die. I've felt half-dead ever since."

"So have I, Goldilocks." He paused. "Maybe I was jumping to conclusions, but after all those calls I'd made, I just thought it was hopeless. I couldn't take—"

"I know. That part was all my fault. You know, Eric, I've never been in love before. I almost hate to admit it, but I didn't know what to do. I didn't know what to believe. I was so naive. I just thought you were using me. I didn't want to be hurt. Susan and I tried to get your address through her father, who knows people in the entertainment business, but he couldn't help, until he came up with the tickets for today. I was almost afraid to come, Eric. Afraid of your reaction. When I found out who you really were, I figured it would be so easy for you to find someone else to take my place. Who am I but just another girl, who doesn't know the first thing about love. . . ."

"Don't say that!" He gripped her hands so that the pressure almost hurt. "You're not just another girl. You're so much more than that. You're wonderful, warm, funny, fun to be with, and beautiful, too, if all the other things aren't enough."

"Eric, do you mean that?"

"I've meant it all along."

"I believed what you said on the beach, but

161

I've been so afraid to trust anything since I found out who you really are."

"Listen, Jena, I wanted to keep things cool, but suddenly I woke up and realized that what I had with you was more important. I knew then that I wanted to find a way to keep our relationship going. It wouldn't have been easy, but that was what I wanted."

Jena closed her eyes as his words sank in.

"I'll be going back to New York in four days."

"That soon?"

"I have to."

"It doesn't have to end."

"How could we see each other?"

Taking her chin in his fingers, he lifted her face. "We'll make a way, Jena. I travel all the time. I can't promise that I can meet you every weekend, but I'm in New York a lot." His brow furrowed suddenly. "But what will your parents think?"

"They'll like you."

"I've made my own success. I'm doing very well, I'll admit, but I'm not the kind of guy most wealthy families would be eager to see lined up with their daughter."

"Why not?"

Eric looked astounded that she didn't understand. "Because I'm in rock music. My profession isn't symbolic of security, high class, or high values."

"But you're not like that."

162

"I know. I come from good roots, and my parents put enough sense in my head so that I came out of it on top. But your average rock musician hasn't left a savory trail behind him."

"My parents aren't like that. They judge people by what they are—not by what they do for a living. If they ever have any objections to my seeing you after they've met you, it will be because they don't want to believe I'm growing up."

"You *are* growing up, Goldilocks." His gaze was so warm, Jena blushed. Then his voice took a more serious note. "I think they know that, Jena. They're just hiding from the truth. If they hadn't thought you were growing up, they would have taken you with them to Europe this year."

"What do you mean?"

"You told me they wouldn't let you go with them, as much as you wanted to, because they thought you were a child and would be happier at the ranch. *I* think they made you stay here because they were afraid you were too much a young lady, too attractive. They were afraid that you'd be exposed to things, become involved in things they weren't ready to have you experience. You understand what I'm saying?"

Jena pursed her lips. "Yes. I understand. They couldn't shoo me off to a hotel room like they used to. I would have wanted to go with them to parties and things."

"They were protecting you."

"They always have. But they have to let me grow up sometime."

"They will. I'm sure when they see you again, they'll realize that. Jena, that's another thing. There's a big difference between us—in experience. Not that I mind. But you should think about it."

"I have already. I know that, unlike you, I haven't been around all that much. I'm still in high school and want to go to college. I want to be somebody in my own right, even if I'm not sure what it is I want to be yet. But that didn't stop us from having a good time this summer. Or from being close."

"No, and it won't stop us from here on in, either. I learned something this summer—about relationships—about myself. Some things are worth going out of your way to protect. *We* have that kind of relationship, and I don't want it to end."

"Neither do I," Jena whispered.

Eric's palms touched her cheeks, then her shoulders, then his arms wrapped around her, pulling her close. He looked down at her, his lips only inches from hers. His eyes said everything.

"I love you, Goldilocks—I do."

"I love you, too."

The wind whistled through the palms that stood, old and everlasting, around them. The buzz of voices could be heard in the distance, drowned out by the music of the gulls calling and circling and the rush of the waves on the beach below. As the setting sun glinted on the windshield, Eric lowered his lips to hers. Jena sighed and gave herself to the warm rush of feeling.

"There are going to be a lot of good times ahead of us," Eric whispered. "So much to do and talk about, so much to discover about each other. And this time we'll be starting out on the right foot. No more lies. I'll never do that to you again."

"I know you won't, Eric."

"We have four days before you leave. I'd like to spend them with you at La Paloma. I'll make the time—if that's OK."

"You know it's OK."

"And this fall. I should be able to get to New York at the end of September. That's not so far away, is it?"

"We can talk to each other in between."

"I'll burn out the phone wires." He smiled softly. "Ah, Goldilocks, what a wonderful ending to a wonderful summer."

Jena nodded, then lifted her lips to his.

(01456-0)   5¼" × 7⅝" $5.95

Now you can have a place to record all your dreams, secret desires and special feelings. The SWEET DREAMS DIARY gives you the perfect opportunity to jot it all down. Plus, it's filled with sayings about love and friendship, poems, and astrological information. The diary is spiral-bound, which makes it easy to write in, no matter where you are.

So order your copy of the SWEET DREAMS DIARY today—and let your friends know about it. In the years to come, you'll be able to look back in your diary and see which of your dreams have come true!

Read these great new *Sweet Dreams* romances, on sale soon:

( ) #29 NEVER LOVE A COWBOY by Jesse DuKore (On sale December 15, 1982 • 23101-4 • $1.95)
Bitsy is thrilled when she moves from crowded New York City to colorful Austin, Texas, and even more thrilled when she sees handsome Billy Joe riding his horse to school. But even when Bitsy's new school radio program grabs everyone else's attention, Billy Joe's eye remains on gorgeous Betty Lou. Can a city girl like Bitsy ever win the heart of a Texas cowboy like Billy Joe?

( ) #30 LITTLE WHITE LIES by Lois T. Fisher (On sale December 15, 1982 • 23102-2 • $1.95)
Everyone says Nina has a good imagination—a gift for telling stories. In fact, it's one of her stories that attracts Scott to her. He's one of the Daltonites, the most sophisticated clique in the school. The Daltonites don't welcome outsiders, but Nina finds it so easy to impress them with a little exaggeration here, a white lie there. But her lies finally start to catch up with her, and Nina's afraid of losing Scott forever.

( ) #31 TOO CLOSE FOR COMFORT by Debra Spector (On sale January 15, 1983 • 23189-8 • $1.95)
For years Drea and Derek have been best friends. They've always loved each other, but when Derek asks Drea for a date, their feelings grow stronger, until finally they're *in love*. Then things start going sour for Drea. Is it because

Derek's becoming so possessive? Or because Sam Henessy's getting interested in her? Should Drea break up with Derek? And if they do, can they ever be friends again?

( ) #32 DAYDREAMER by Janet Quin-Harkin (On sale January 15, 1983 • 23190-1 • $1.95)
All too often, Lisa finds herself escaping into daydreams—dreams of fame, friends and boyfriends galore, Hollywood, her parents, and falling in love. But when her fantasy bubble bursts, she has to open her eyes to the fact that, in real life, things don't always work out the way they do in dreams.

( ) THE LOVE BOOK by Deidre Laiken & Alan Schneider (On sale January 15, 1983 • 23288-6 • $1.95)
If people could recognize true love at first glance, life (and love) would be a lot less complicated. But love is not always what it appears to be. The more you know about love, the more successful you'll be at finding and keeping it—and understanding love is what this, the first nonfiction *Sweet Dreams* book, is all about.

Buy these books at your local bookstore or use this handy coupon for ordering:

You'll fall in love with all the Sweet Dream romances. Reading these stories, you'll be reminded of yourself or of someone you know. There's Jennie, the *California Girl*, who becomes an outsider when her family moves to Texas. And Cindy, the *Little Sister*, who's afraid that Christine, the oldest in the family, will steal her new boyfriend. Don't miss any of the Sweet Dreams romances.

☐	22542	**LOVE SONG #19** Anne park	$1.95
☐	22682	**THE POPULARITY SUMMER #20** Rosemary Vernon	$1.95
☐	22607	**ALL'S FAIR IN LOVE #21** Jeanne Andrews	$1.95
☐	22683	**SECRET IDENTITY #22** Joanna Campbell	$1.95
☐	22840	**FALLING IN LOVE AGAIN #23** Barbara Conklin	$1.95
☐	22957	**THE TROUBLE WITH CHARLIE #24** Jaye Ellen	$1.95
☐	22543	**HER SECRET SELF #25** Rhondi Villot	$1.95
☐	22692	**IT MUST BE MAGIC #26** Marian Woodruff	$1.95
☐	22681	**TOO YOUNG FOR LOVE #27** Gailanne Maravel	$1.95
☐	23053	**TRUSTING HEARTS #28** Jocelyn Saal	$1.95

Buy them at your local bookstore or use this handy coupon for ordering:

Bantam Books, Inc., Dept. SD, 414 East Golf Road, Des Plaines, Ill. 60016

Please send me the books I have checked above. I am enclosing
$_____ (please add $1.25 to cover postage and handling). Send
check or money order—no cash or C.O.D.'s please.

Mr/Mrs/Miss_____

Address_____

City _____ State/Zip _____

SD-12/82

Please allow four to six weeks for delivery. This offer expires 6/83.